As Time Goes By

Tales from Grace Chapel Inn®

As Time Goes By

Annie Jones

Guideposts

NEW YORK, NEW YORK

Acknowledgments

All Scripture quotations are taken from
The Holy Bible, New International Version. Copyright © 1973,
1978, 1984 International Bible Society. Used by permission
of Zondervan Bible Publishers.

www.guideposts.com
(800) 431-2344
Guideposts Books & Inspirational Media
Series Editors: Regina Hersey and Leo Grant
Cover art by Edgar Jerins
Cover design by Wendy Bass
Interior design by Cindy LaBreacht
Typeset by Nancy Tardi
Printed in the United States of America

Acknowledgments

Thank you to the good people at Guideposts, especially Regina Hersey, and to everyone who encouraged and helped to make this book come to be.

In loving memory of Gerald.

—Annie Jones

Chapter One

"Should auld acquaintance be forgot and never brought to mind. . . ." Ethel Howard Buckley marched into the parlor of Grace Chapel Inn in full voice and carrying an empty storage carton.

"It's almost suppertime on New Year's Day, Aunt Ethel. I'd say it's long past the hour to be singing that."

Ethel had a decent sense of pitch and a robust delivery that Louise might, on some occasions, have admired from a woman of her aunt's seventy-plus years. However, it had been a long, busy day, and Louise did yearn for a bit of quiet.

"It's not as though there were an expiration date on the tune." Ethel plunked down the carton at Louise's feet. Then, with a mischievous gleam in her eyes, she held up one hand and moved her finger along as if reading from an unseen label. "Best if sung before noon on New Year's Day."

Louise chuckled softly and then stepped back to eye the last remnant of the Christmas season in their home, the tree. With her younger sister Alice filling in for another nurse at the hospital in Potterston today and her youngest sister Jane in the kitchen working on a special New Year's Day meal, the task of removing the holiday decorations had fallen primarily to Louise this year. "I'm just in a peculiar mood today, Aunt Ethel. I always find it a bit sad when the holiday season is coming to a close."

"But don't forget that means the New Year with all its wonderful potential is off to a roaring start." Ethel clapped her hands to show she was already excited to see what the coming year would bring.

"So true." Louise took a moment to study the tree before adding, "Yet, taking down the decorations seems to put the finish on all the holiday fun."

"Are you sad, dear?" Ethel asked with genuine concern in her sweet voice.

"No, not sad, really."

She glanced around the parlor. They had chosen that room to put up the tree because, in the days after Thanksgiving, it had seemed the perfect setting. Back then, the weather forecasters were predicting a typical cold and snowy Pennsylvania December for the Acorn Hill area. Louise, Alice and Jane had hoped the cozy ambiance of this particular room would delight the guests and visitors throughout the season.

"Well, what then?"

"I'm just remembering what wonderful expectations we had for these holidays, sitting around a crackling fire, sipping warm cider or cocoa, " Louise said softly as she gazed at the nearly perfect setting they had created.

Louise recalled what Alice had said when they first started the decorating. "Won't it be wonderful to gather for caroling practice in the parlor with a fire blazing in the fireplace, casting low lights around the room and making the crystal chandelier sparkle?"

The image evoked a homespun charm, but it had never became a reality. Acorn Hill and the surrounding region had experienced one of the warmest Decembers on record.

Louise touched a tree branch. "With no snow nor much cold weather, it just didn't seem like the holidays."

"That suited me just fine. I could do with a little less *brrr* and *t-t-t*-teeth chattering." Ethel laced her arms in front of her yellow and orange print dress and feigned a shiver.

"Well, it made the season seem a bit lacking to me. No, not lacking," Louise corrected herself almost instantly in order to substitute a better description. "Lackluster."

"*Hmm.*" The silence followed was broken only a moment later when Ethel added, "But now that it's almost over, let the New Year begin!"

"Now that it's almost over." Louise's gaze fell to the storage boxes that lay at her feet.

The scent of pine from the holiday greenery had all but disappeared from the air.

Alice would be home from her shift at the hospital soon, probably full of cheer and whatever goodies the staff had brought in to share.

Jane was in the kitchen concocting a hearty meal to use up the leftover ham and who knew what else.

Their aunt had come over from her home in the carriage house next door this morning to help Louise. She mostly had spent the day peering out the windows to check on people passing by and pointing out what needed to be taken down while not making any move to do so herself.

Removing the Christmas decorations had become, with each passing year, more and more of a sweet, yet poignant, task for sixty-five-year-old Louise. It gave her time to recount the blessings of fun and family as they celebrated together this past year, of course, but she also thought back to Christmases that had gone before.

So many objects held a special place in her memory. Some evoked the joy and wonder of childhood, both hers, her sisters' and her daughter's. Others carried with them the reminder of the life she had shared with her dear, late husband Eliot Smith.

She savored the memories of those who no longer gathered

with them for services on Christmas Eve or at the table for Christmas dinner, whether because of separations of earthly miles or eternal passing.

"... and never brought to mind ...," Ethel was singing softly as she drifted around the room.

Louise reached out and plucked off an old family ornament, a silver ball with a glittery scene of a snow-covered church on one side. In this she saw her mother.

Madeleine Howard had loved the simple adornment. Each year she brought it out of its special container and held it up for Louise and Alice to admire. Every year she told them the story about how their father had given it to her before they were married and how she had felt that by looking into it she was seeing their future together. She would point to the image and tell of seeing them as husband and wife, of seeing him becoming the pastor of a wonderful church where they would both serve the Lord.

With that, she would hold up the ball and ask the girls what they saw. To which they would cry, "Me!"

"I see myself."

"I see Alice."

"I see Louise!"

"That's right." Mother would laugh. "I looked into this ornament and saw my future, and there you are—right there!"

The honor of hanging the memento on the tree had gone to Louise the year after her mother died. It still made her throat close up a bit to remember how she had stood on tiptoe to place it delicately near the top where it would look down on all of them, especially their baby sister Jane. There it would remind them that even though their mother was gone, her love for them, their father and the Lord still shone over them always.

"'... we'll take a cup of kindness yet ...'"

Later, when Louise had married, the job passed to Alice

and then to Jane when Alice was in nursing school and occasionally couldn't get home for Christmas. Then it went back to Alice when Jane went to art school in San Francisco. Now that they were all back home running a bed-and-breakfast, Grace Chapel Inn, in their family home, they had decided they would select the spot together.

Hanging that special ornament was a touching moment for them all. It always led to stories about the year Jane did this or Alice did that. When their father was still with them, those recollections had delighted him so.

"For auld lang syne."

"Father," Louise murmured under her breath. Rev. Daniel Joseph Howard. She saw *him* and her own daughter Cynthia in the imperfect papier-mâché crèche Cynthia had made him. With figures shaped by small hands into neckless camels, angels with lopsided wings and Mary with bright yellow yarn hair, the nativity scene had always been treated by Daniel Howard like something made of the most precious materials in the world. Which it was, of course, because it was made with love.

To see her husband, all Louise needed to do was to look at the piano and the tattered old book of Christmas carols that he had loved to hear her play. Her heart filled with tenderness and gratitude for the time they had shared.

Should auld acquaintance be forgot?

Louise did not need to ponder that question long. She carried these people, and so many others, with her daily in her thoughts, her prayers and her heart. She prayed for those still with her and looked forward to the day when she would see in heaven those who had gone before her.

Ethel's singing was like a continuous tape. Once she reached the end of the song, she began over again.

"Aunt Ethel, if you wish to sing, why not choose something more upbeat?"

"*More* upbeat? I always thought of *that* song as cheery."

"Cheery? Really? It's so very sentimental, though. It makes me quite nostalgic."

"Sentimental?" Ethel made a sputtering sound and gave a light wave of her hand. "It puts me in mind of paper hats and horns and shouting 'Happy New Year!' while people toss confetti into the air. I never thought of that as nostalgic at all."

"Well, that may be how people sing it nowadays, I suppose." Louise brushed her fingertips over the sparkling church scene on the ornament in her other hand. "But in truth, it's quite nostalgic, quite sentimental. The very name has an aching sense of longing to it."

"Is that so?" Ethel tipped her head to one side and puzzled over the idea for a moment. "Auld . . . Lang . . . Syne? I'm not even sure I know what that means, precisely."

"Long time since." Louise put the delicate glass ball away in its special box and then added it to the carton of ornaments.

"*Hmm?*" Ethel looked bewildered.

"The translation of 'Auld Lang Syne' is 'long time since,'" she explained as she went on with her work. "More colloquially, one might say it means 'days gone by.' It's a Scottish phrase from a poem by Robert Burns."

"Burns, yes. We had to learn his poems as memory pieces in grammar school," Ethel noted.

"The melody is what's called a pentatonic folk song," Louise said. "I'm sure I have the words on some sheet music if you want to try to decipher them."

"Oh no, dear. I have enough on my hands just deciphering your explanation." The older woman threw up her hands and laughed.

Louise nodded, happy to accept the gentle ribbing. "I'll put it more simply, then, Aunt Ethel. To me that song has always been akin to a prayer that I find myself saying more and more."

"A prayer?"

"Yes." Louise moved to her aunt's side and sat on the corner of the chair. "A plea to the Lord to remember and minister to anyone that my more and more faulty brain may have forgotten but who remains in my heart."

"I wish I could say I don't know what you mean by that," Ethel tapped the side of her head. "Some days I think I have forgotten more than I ever knew."

Louise put her hand on her aunt's arm. "So you can see why I'd think of that song as a simple prayer. One offered to give thanks for all the people who have blessed my life and whose lives I wish to ask blessings for as well."

"Oh, Louise, what a lovely thought." Ethel paused and placed her hand above her heart. "I think I'm going to like that song so much more now."

Louise gave her aunt another pat; then she rose and reached to take a golden bird's nest with a handblown glass cardinal in it from a low branch of the tree. "From a party-goer's song to a prayer of remembrance in just a few sentences? That's quite a leap, Aunt Ethel."

"As leaps go, it wasn't all that much, dear. You put it so well. Besides, the idea of looking at things in a new way, of doing things differently this coming year, beginning with how and why we pray are subjects that have been on my mind all week, ever since the Rev. Thompson's sermon last Sunday."

"Yes, that sermon made quite an impression on me too. Alice and Jane both mentioned it as well."

Rev. Kenneth Thompson had begun by asking them all to say the Lord's Prayer together with him, not to rush through the words they knew by rote, but actually to pray the words as Jesus taught.

"I liked that quote at the end of the sermon, the one that he said he got from a test canister."

"A test . . . ?" Louise frowned for only a moment before she put the pieces together and chuckled softly. "Oh no,

Aunt Ethel. Not a test canister, a *desk calendar*. He was paraphrasing a quote he'd seen on a church secretary's calendar many years ago."

"A desk calendar? Oh, why yes. Yes, that does make much more sense."

Louise considered asking her aunt just what she had imagined a test canister was, but then thought better of it. Knowing Ethel, Louise realized that she had probably cobbled together what seemed to her a perfectly logical description of just such an item and why their pastor would have had access to one. Louise didn't want to break the special feeling of the moment they had just shared with a discussion like that.

So she set another decoration in the tissue-lined box and said, "I wrote down the quotation so that I could meditate on it later. Alice and Jane both asked me for a copy of it as well, so I have it pretty firmly set in my memory."

Louise shut her eyes, concentrating on getting the words as close to what she had transcribed as possible.

> "The sweetest prayers our Lord does hear,
> that are of greatest beauty,
> are not those when we ask for things,
> but just report for duty."

"'Just report for duty.'" Ethel gave a nod and then leaned back in her chair. "I learn more things when I come over here, Louise. First about 'Auld Lang Syne.' Then that thoughtful little quote. I can't imagine what I will pick up next."

Chapter Two

As Louise finished packing the tree ornaments, a spirited call came from Jane as she made her way from the kitchen to the parlor. "Hoppin' John is almost ready, y'all."

"Hopping who?" Ethel looked questioningly at Louise.

"Y'all?" Louise repeated with a shrug.

Jane appeared at the doorway of the parlor with a smile on her face. Though she was enveloped in a white chef's apron, she had a festive look, having tied her glossy brown ponytail with a lovely poinsettia print scarf. "Hoppin' John. Ham and beans served with piping hot corn bread and greens. It's a Southern tradition to prepare this meal on New Year's Day in hopes that it will bring prosperity and good fortune for the coming year."

"It sounds hearty and delicious." Ethel said. "Even though it isn't cold out, it seems right to have comfort food at this time of year."

"I agree, Auntie. I read about the dish in a cooking magazine and thought it might be fun to try it." Jane was all about trying new things, having fun and always, always about good taste, both in the flavor of her food and the way she applied her creative flair to everything from the clothes she wore to her home decor. "I'm just trying what Kenneth urged us all to do in last Sunday's sermon—to approach the coming year with a renewed commitment to serving the Lord with our hearts, minds and talents."

"That's what you took away from that sermon?" Ethel cocked her head and held out her hand, wordlessly asking for her youngest niece to help her up from the soft chair in which she had ensconced herself. "Louise was just saying she thought it was about a new way of singing 'Auld Lang Syne.'"

Jane looked in surprise to Louise, leaving Ethel in mid-rise for a moment.

Louise clarified what she had actually said. "I took more to heart the part about the nature of prayer."

"Jane, sweetheart, did you know our pastor was reading from a desk calendar, not a test canister?" It took Ethel a moment to get steady on her feet.

Observing Jane's puzzled look, Louise whispered, "I'll tell you about that later." Then she cleared her throat and said aloud, "Perhaps this Hopping John dish that Jane's made will be just the thing to fuel a lively conversation about that sermon."

"Hoppin'," Jane said, enunciating the word slowly, pointedly ending it with an *n*. "It's Southern, y'all."

"Well, as long as it tastes good, I'll be happy," Ethel announced.

"Oh, and I'm certainly up for any kind of lively discussion." Jane led the way toward the kitchen. "Though I doubt it can change my opinion that the central message of Sunday's sermon was that we must rise to the challenge of the future and not be afraid to try new things."

"As long as you don't throw the baby out with the bathwater when you do," Ethel warned.

"Oh, Aunt Ethel, I hardly ever use bathwater in my recipes," Jane said with a wink at Louise.

Ethel opened her mouth to respond, alarm in her eyes. Then, before she could say a word, her expression softened as she got the joke. She closed her mouth and shook her head at Jane's silliness. "I meant that too often people rush to latch onto the latest trend or newfangled way of doing something and forget that the way it has been done for a long time isn't so bad, either."

"That's a wise observation," Louise said as she followed her sister and aunt toward the kitchen. "People are too quick to dismiss the tried and true for the fast and fashionable these days."

Jane glanced back over her shoulder, looking at Louise, and asked, "Not too keen on new things, eh? Does that mean you two won't be sampling any Hoppin' John?"

"Oh no," Louise said as she entered the kitchen and sniffed the aroma arising from the stove. "That smells too good to miss."

Louise and Ethel took seats at the table, looking forward to a delicious new eating experience.

"Good. I think you'll like the meal. It's simple but tasty, especially when served with corn bread."

The cozy kitchen was moist with steam from the concoction simmering on the stove.

Jane went over to the door that led to the small back porch, opened it and swung it a few times to circulate some fresh air through the warm room. "I timed the bread to come out of the oven about the same time Alice should be getting home from work."

"Work." Ethel clucked her tongue. "I don't know why she didn't just stay home today."

"The hospital is short staffed, and she is always happy to pitch in when she's needed," Jane said, fanning the door another time or two before closing it.

Just then the front door opened and then closed.

"Hello?" Alice called out. "I'm home."

"We're in the kitchen, dear," Ethel responded before anyone else could reply.

A cheery little "ding" from the oven timer sang out the news that the corn bread was done.

"Right on cue." Jane turned on her heel and headed across the black-and-white checkerboard floor toward the oven. "The corn bread will have to cool for a few minutes. Then it's time for Hoppin' John."

"Hop and John?" Alice breezed into the kitchen, her cheeks flushed and her reddish-brown hair only slightly out of place from the early evening breeze. "Do we have guests for dinner?"

"Hoppin' John," Louise pronounced it properly this time, which meant she pronounced it quite *im*properly to her way of thinking. "Jane is serving a traditional Southern New Year's dish."

"Hang up your coat and grab a seat. I'll serve it as soon as the corn bread cools." Jane raised the pan of dense, cake-like yellow bread for all to see.

"Wonderful." Alice hung her coat on a hook by the back door. "I don't know why I even bothered with a coat today. For the short walk to and from my car, it was warm enough just for my uniform."

"How was your day?" Louise asked.

"Interesting." Alice turned and paused a moment before adding, "Thought-provoking."

"Thought-provoking?"

"Let's just say I had reason to mull over last Sunday's sermon on how even though we may begin with a childlike faith, we must never stop learning and building on that faith."

"Were we all hearing the same sermon last Sunday?" Jane wondered aloud.

"I heard that while we may begin with the Lord's Prayer, taught to us as children, as we grow, each part of that prayer should take on new meaning. We should trust the Lord for our daily needs, turn to Him when faced with temptation and be ready when we hear His call. In other words, we must not just repeat the familiar words about His will being done but take them to heart and live them."

"Well! All this reflection is leading me to make a New Year's resolution right here and now."

The sisters looked at their aunt.

She held up her hand as if taking a solemn oath and announced, "From now on, I am taking notes in church."

"Good for you, Aunt Ethel." Alice bent down and gave the older woman a quick hug around the shoulders. "You certainly look pretty in those bright colors. They set off your red hair. Have you been here long?"

"All day," Jane and Louise said together, and then smiled a bit shamefacedly. They loved their aunt—truly they did—but a full day with her tended to feel like, well, a *full* day.

"We've been *un*decorating," Ethel informed Alice.

"Why yes, I can see. The place looks almost normal again." Alice made a quick survey of the room around them. "I hope you didn't overdo."

"Aunt Ethel supervised, mostly." Louise smiled at her sister.

"And provided some much-needed background music." Ethel beamed.

"I'm sorry I missed out on the fun." Alice said with a laugh.

"You certainly are in a cheerful mood, especially for somebody who had to work on a holiday," Ethel observed.

"Oh, it wasn't too taxing. Besides, I *like* working on New Year's Day. I like knowing I've done my part to allow people who have small children or visiting relatives to spend more time with them." Alice took a seat. "And I confess that I enjoy the excitement of seeing if the first baby of the New Year will be born during my shift."

"And?" Jane asked.

"A boy. Born on an earlier shift— shortly after three this morning. Everyone was still buzzing about him when I started work."

"What is his name?" Ethel asked.

"I don't know. We're calling him Baby New Year."

"I can just imagine him now with that banner and a tiny top hat." Jane sank a knife into the corn bread and in doing so released its rich aroma into the air.

"Don't you usually call newborns by the parents' last name? Baby Boy Buckley, for example."

"Aunt Ethel, I can't tell you the last name because the parents have asked that their name be withheld. They don't want it in the paper even though that usually means they would get some gifts from local merchants."

"Oh?" Louise said.

"But what about the first name? They must have given the child a first name?" Ethel insisted.

"No, actually they haven't. Not yet. Because . . ." Alice looked down for a moment. "You all know I would never share details about a patient, but I can tell you that he was premature and there is concern about his prognosis."

"Prognosis?" Ethel frowned.

Alice placed her hand over her aunt's. "They aren't sure if he will make it, Aunt Ethel."

"Oh. Oh dear. No." The older woman's eyes pooled with tears.

"If he makes progress through the next few days, then he will probably be fine. He won't leave the hospital for some time, but he will be fine." Alice paused a moment as if considering whether to say more. Finally her shoulders slumped slightly and she added, "The parents are young. Their own parents are on the West Coast. They only have friends from work in town and, like a lot of young people, have no one to step in and guide them, no church home. I feel so sorry for them."

"Perhaps our church could organize something," Louise said. "A collection? Someone to counsel them?"

"I have no idea about their finances or insurance situation." Alice shook her head. "But the rest is all being handled through different people at the hospital and that's all the parents will accept—whatever comes through the hospital."

"I wish there were something more we could do," Jane brought a basket of freshly cut corn bread to the table, set it down and then put her hand on Alice's shoulder in a show of support.

"Oh, but Jane, there is." Alice smiled up at her younger sister. "We can pray."

"Yes, we can pray." Louise felt a surge of hope. "We *should* pray. Not just to ask God's mercy on the child and his parents but also because it's the right way to start the New Year."

The sisters and their aunt joined hands. Louise prayed aloud for the child in need and his parents. She prayed for each one at the table that she find peace and purpose in the coming year. She closed the prayer with the plea, "Here we are, Lord, send us. We will answer Your call. Your will be done. Amen."

"Amen," Jane and Alice murmured in unison.

"Amen," Aunt Ethel came in a beat behind.

Chapter Three

The phone rang at the inn precisely at nine o'clock the next morning, and a man with an oddly quick-paced Southern accent asked to speak to Jane. *Miss* Jane, actually.

"This *is* Jane speaking," she informed the man. There was something familiar about his voice and she tried to place it. "How may I help you?"

"I don't know if you recall making my acquaintance, ma'am. The name is Sturgis, Lyndon Sturgis."

"Sturgis? Lyndon Sturgis," Jane repeated the name slowly. "Your voice is certainly familiar, but I am having trouble placing the name. How would I have made your acquaintance, Mr. Sturgis?"

"Me and my late wife Barbie stayed with y'all at your pretty little inn there in Acorn Hill a while back. We used it as a home base, as it were, for traipsing to and fro to Merriville on the occasion of my only daughter's wedding."

"Ah yes. The wedding. It was so lovely. And you and . . . excuse me, did you just say your *late* wife?"

"Yes. I did. Sadly my sweetheart of thirty-five years passed away not long after our visit with you."

"I am so sorry to hear that, Mr. Sturgis. She seemed so kindhearted and was so pleasant."

"She was that and so much more," he agreed. "I miss her every day and all the more now with the wonderful news that our daughter is going to have a baby."

"Congratulations."

"It's a blessing all right, and so is the fact that our son-in-law is going into his family's business."

"His family? In Merriville?" Now the pieces were beginning to come together. "So, you want to book a room to come for a visit?"

"I actually wanted to talk to you because of how you went all out for me and Barbie, not to mention our daughter and her whole wedding party."

"I appreciated your inviting me and my friend Sylvia Songer to attend."

"That was the least we could do, seeing as how you did so much to help us with last-minute details and refused to take a cent for your efforts."

"It was our pleasure," she said. Though Lyndon Sturgis had often been difficult to work with, in the end he deserved the phrase he had used to describe the people of Acorn Hill, "just plain good folks."

"And that friend of yours proved mighty handy whipping up the hem on Barbie's mother-of-the-bride dress, though for a minute or two I thought we were going to have to make her an honorary member of the wedding party."

Jane laughed at the thought of poor Sylvia still stitching and tying the thread in a knot even as the music rose to cue Mrs. Sturgis that it was time for her to be seated. If Jane remembered correctly, Mr. Sturgis had refused to pay the store where they had purchased the dress to do the hem, insisting his wife could do it herself. But with the rush and confusion of long-distance wedding preparations, she had taken up the hem very hurriedly at the last moment. Arriving just before the ceremony, she noticed a thread hanging from the skirt of her dress and pulled it. The entire hem came out. Mr. Sturgis had offered Sylvia three times as much as he would have paid the store's seamstress if she'd sew up the hem then and there. Sylvia had refused any compensation, of course, and had saved the day with her quick and expert work.

"I hope that your son-in-law's best man has gotten over my tendency to revert to a polka every time he tried to teach me the Texas Two-Step."

The man on the other end of the line laughed. "I'm sure he didn't mind one bit, you being such a gracious and elegant dance partner. Which is why I gave you a call today."

"I beg your pardon?"

"Oh, not to be anyone's dance partner, but because you are a lady with a sense of elegance and good taste, and you don't mind getting your hands dirty."

"Thank you, I think. But I don't quite understand—"

"I want to hire you."

"Hire? Oh, you mean you want to cater a meal?"

"Meal? No. Nothing like that. I'll pay you, of course."

"What are you offering to pay me *for*, Mr. Sturgis?"

"Didn't I tell you?"

"No."

"My daughter and her husband are moving from Texas to Merriville."

"Yes, that much I understood."

"Because of that I intend to have myself a second house in the Acorn Hill area so I can come and visit whenever I get a mind to. And I want you to help me make that house a reality."

"Lyndon Sturgis?" Louise asked shortly after Jane had hung up the phone and joined her and Alice in the kitchen. "Should I remember him?"

"How could you forget him?" Alice said, countered with a twinkle of merry mischief in her eyes. "He and his wife stayed here a year or so ago."

"He told me that his wife died shortly after their visit here," Jane informed her sisters.

"Oh, I'm so sorry to hear that," Alice said. "I don't recall much about her, other than that she was very quiet."

"How sad," Louise said, then shook her head, clearly still unable to remember the man in question.

"Their daughter was marrying a boy from Merriville and they came up from Texas and stayed the week of the wedding." Jane had so enjoyed pitching in with last-minute details for the festivities, including arranging for Craig Tracy to step in and do the wedding flowers when the original florist was taken ill. Working with them, she had gotten to know the couple much better than either Alice or Louise. "To be fair, they were gone more than they were here, so you shouldn't feel too bad about not remembering him."

"Oh, she remembers him," Alice assured them. "She just needs the right cue to trigger her memory. Does this sound familiar?" Perching herself on the edge of her chair, Alice puffed herself up and intoned, "Ladies, I don't mind paying for the things that I want. But I want the full measure of what I pay for."

"Oh!" Louise said. "The . . . the tall gentleman who insisted on being served soda in an unopened can with an empty glass and ice cubes in a bowl?"

"That's the one." Jane nodded.

"The soda business was nothing compared to the tea bags." Alice launched into her engaging but not the least bit malicious imitation of the man once again. "This business of one cup of tea per bag is nonsense. You can easily get three cups out of a bag and anything less is as wasteful as that there Boston Tea Party."

"Yes. It's all coming back now," Louise said with a smile.

"Alice, you are in rare form today," Jane teased.

Alice shrugged and wrinkled her nose in delight. "You know I don't mean anything by it. I sincerely enjoy all our guests, quirks and foibles and all."

"Maybe it's my age talking," Louise said, "but I have no quibble with this Mr. Sturgis' viewpoint. Generally speaking."

"Really?" Since she was about to get involved in dealings with the man, Jane wanted to hear her sister's opinion on this.

"Yes. Too many people have forgotten what generations before us have gone through." Louise frowned. "They've cast aside the lessons of good stewardship in favor of convenience. They are often too quick to discard things that could be salvaged, made whole again."

"I understand what you mean, Louise. I saw so much waste in the restaurant business. And I really didn't mind Mr. Sturgis' eccentricities. I appreciated his candor and clarity because it made it easier for me to give him the best service and not waste my own time or effort."

"That's certainly something I can understand. Good time management is a skill I try to emphasize to new nurses."

"People need to feel productive. That's another given of good stewardship," Louise said. "They need not just to serve, but to serve with purpose."

"That's a wonderful thought, Louise," Alice said before turning to Jane and asking, "And that brings a question to my mind: What is your purpose going to be in all this, Jane?"

"To be honest, he's not really sure. I sort of think that since he's trying to do something like this for the first time ever without his wife, he just wants a woman's input."

"On what?"

"That's what I am going to go find out now. He made

that phone call from his car. He has driven up from Texas and will be in town in an hour." Jane raised a coffee cup to her lips, paused and shook her head in mild disbelief over her own actions. "I probably should have gotten more details before I agreed to it. I just don't know what made me say yes."

"Perhaps it was the influence of the delicious recipe you made last night. It made you favorable to all things Southern," Alice suggested.

"Does that mean you really liked the touch of Southern cuisine?"

"It was very tasty." Alice said. "I can see how it got you *hoppin'* into all this."

"I think it might be because in our prayer we pledged to serve wherever we are needed," Louise reminded them.

"Yes, of course." Jane tipped her head to one side. "It's just that . . ."

"What?" Alice asked.

Jane sighed, and let her shoulders sag. "Only when we said that prayer, I assumed it would mean we'd be pitching in with this helpless little baby."

"Ah."

"I pictured myself buying darling little outfits and seeing if Sylvia would do a quilt for the nursery." Sylvia made lovely quilts. Jane could imagine that together they might come up with a creation that would be serviceable and a keepsake for a lifetime. "Not to mention the ideas that started churning in my brain for fund-raising events to help out those poor young parents."

"Only those poor young parents don't want charity events and attention. As I told you, they will only accept help that comes through the hospital. So, really, you shouldn't be surprised that when you have a chance to do something to help someone, it comes from another direction."

"Yes, yes. It's just that, well, baby clothes and a keepsake quilt seem so much more . . ."

"You never know when a simple kindness or small show of support might make all the difference, Jane," Louise said. "Helping a stranger find a home in a new place—you have no idea what doors that might open or how the Lord might use that."

"Still, maybe at some point the family will be open to outside help and Sylvia and I can make that quilt."

Alice brushed her shoulder affectionately against her younger sister's, using just enough contact to jostle Jane into a slow and self-deprecating smile at her reluctance to give up on her initial idea of how she would fulfill her commitment to serve. "You heard the sermon as well as we did, Jane. You study and prepare, you do what you know you should, you put into practice everything you learn, and when God calls, you will be ready to answer, no matter what is asked of you."

"Now see, that is not what I got from that at all." Jane lowered her coffee cup and crinkled her brow thoughtfully. "Well, not exactly. I came away with a conviction that our prayer life should ready us to tackle new things. That we must step out of our old ways, and prayer and faith will support and guide us."

"Try new things, eh?"

The sisters' gazes met.

Alice pressed her lips together to keep from laughing at Jane's having admitted that she had actually gotten precisely what she had bargained for.

"It's not about what we want, Jane. It's about what God wants from us, and for us. That's what we must be ready to act upon," Louise reminded her with a loving tone.

"Well said!" Alice exclaimed.

Jane nodded her agreement, and then went upstairs to get ready to meet Lyndon Sturgis and see what she could do to help him.

"Howdy there, ma'am. Glad to make your *re*acquaintance." Lyndon Sturgis came strolling up the sidewalk toward Jane as she waited outside the Realtor's office, his hand already outstretched.

Tall, even to Jane's five-feet nine, and dressed in a gray and black Western-cut sports coat, dark casual slacks and cowboy boots, Sturgis was instantly recognizable.

"Hello. It's wonderful to see you again, Mr. Sturgis."

"Lyndon, ma'am." He swept his cowboy hat from his head.

The old-fashioned gesture was not wasted on Jane, who found it quite charming. She did not, however, feel the same about the way he chose to address her. Had she really become the kind of matronly type that even a mature man would address as *ma'am*?

"Lyndon is the name my dear mama gave me, and since we're going to be working so close on this here project, I'd be proud to have you call me by it."

"I'll be happy to use your Christian name, provided you never call me *ma'am* again," Jane said with a laugh. "It makes me feel like an old lady."

"In Texas that's just a courtesy, ma'a . . . um, that is, Ms. Howard."

"Jane." She took his proffered hand and gave it a firm and welcoming shake.

"Jane." He returned her handshake and added a gentlemanly tip of his head. "Thank you for coming out to meet me this morning. I know it is a bit off the cuff to call you as I am rolling into town, but I just got my daughter's news at Christmas, and then her husband's family told them about how fair the weather was up here. Well, you know what they say about striking while the iron is hot."

"Hot? The housing market in Acorn Hill?" Jane asked in a way she thought would coax him into elaborating on that.

Lyndon Sturgis was not one to be coaxed into anything, apparently. He just kept right on talking as if she had never spoken a word. "Not an easy trip, no, but then without my sweet Barbie along, I didn't see the need to dillydally around with stopping for fancy meals or staying in hotels, not when I have a vehicle rugged enough for the long haul but comfortable enough to make a fine shelter for the night." He indicated an enormous silver SUV parked just a few feet away. "Fully loaded with everything a man needs, navigational system, DVD player, the works. Ain't technology a wonderful thing?"

"Yes, in the proper context it can be a lifesaver," Jane said.

"That's for sure. Real time-saver."

"Yes, yes, technology certainly can save lots of time. Still, I tend to think of it more in terms of how it makes life better, which is why I said *life*saver." She felt compelled to point that out, not to be contrary but because she feared that Lyndon was not a very good listener. "On many occasions there are more important things than saving time, I think. Don't you agree?"

"Sure. Whatever you say, but this ain't one of *them* occasions. So we'd better scoot. I'm working under specific time constraints." He gave her a friendly but determined nudge and pointed toward his waiting SUV.

His impatience made Jane hesitate. "Aren't we going into the real estate office?"

"Done that already." He took her by the elbow, ever the

gentleman, but quite clearly the *hurried* gentleman. "Can't afford to dither around. Not when the weather is so cooperative and time's a-wasting. After all, time *is* money. Don't you agree?"

"Oh, I don't know." Jane slipped her elbow gently from his grip. She gave him a polite nod of deference and then swept her hand out to indicate he should lead the way to his vehicle as she said, "Benjamin Franklin once said, 'Dost thou love life? Then do not squander time, for that's the stuff life is made of.' So some might argue that time is not money, but that it is life itself."

"All the more reason not to waste it then, eh?" He leaned forward, gave her a sturdy pat on the back and chuckled. "Let's get going. I have a whole list of places to see."

"You already have all the addresses of places you want to see? If you'd like, I can go over them and tell you what I know about them and then give you the most direct route to them."

"No need. I'll just program in the addresses and wait for the directions to pop up on that little screen on my dashboard. Now there's a piece of time-saving technology you can't take exception to. Think of all the daylight hours we might have lost looking up places and all the gas we might have burned searching them out.

Jane laughed. "Lyndon, this is Acorn Hill. There isn't anyplace you'd need to go here that I couldn't get you to just like that." Jane snapped her fingers.

"Now, see, that's good to know. Makes me feel like I made a right smart choice in asking for your help." With that he opened the car door for her to climb in. "It will be a pleasure working with you, Jane."

She gave him a courteous nod of thanks and fastened her seatbelt as he closed her door, walked around the front of the car and got in the driver's side. He removed his hat, placed it carefully on the backseat, and then buckled up. He put the key in the ignition and then began flipping switches, adjusting things. He plugged in his cell phone to charge it, turned on his global positioning device and flipped off the old style country-and-western crooner *yodel-lee-oh-lay-ing* from the speakers of his satellite radio. All the while, he talked.

And talked.

And talked.

Jane thought when she described him to Sylvia later she would say he looked less like an iconic Western cowboy figure and more like a rain barrel on stilts. He swaggered as he walked, more as a function of his build than of his personality. Though he did seem to possess a propensity for bluster, he had an affable charm about him.

When he spoke of his late wife and daughter, his eyes lit up. Then when he talked about the reason for the sudden push to have a second home up north, the new grandbaby due to be born in the spring, he beamed.

"Told me Christmas morning. A double whammy. Not only did my daughter and her husband have a baby on the way, they were planning to leave Texas so that he can go back to work for his father in Merriville."

"You must have been in shock."

"You could say that, but before I could even process it all, my daughter told me I should move *with* them. 'What is holding you here, Daddy?' she said." He shook his head. "I looked around at the home I had shared with Barbie all those years and thought, 'Well, plenty.' I have friends there, and though I've retired, I have my business interests. And I have my memories. I was not ready to pick up stakes and move away from all that."

"As someone who moved from her longtime home, I completely understand." And in that moment Jane did understand. Lyndon didn't want to listen to her. He wanted to *talk* to her. He was taking this huge step without his late wife and he wanted a sounding board. And it didn't hurt if that sounding board could serve as a conduit to smooth his way into his new home away from home, Acorn Hill.

"But my little girl pleaded with me. She didn't want her baby growing up only seeing me at Christmas. By that afternoon I knew I had to have a second home up north."

"So why did you choose Acorn Hill and not Merriville?" If the man wanted to talk, she would help him find things to talk about that might help her to help him.

"His family lives in Merriville, so I thought moving there would be a bit like intruding. Acorn Hill is far enough away to stay out from underfoot and yet close enough that maybe now and again they might let me take the little one for an overnight visit. And I really took a liking to this small town when we stayed here during the week of the wedding."

"We enjoyed having you and Barbie."

"Barbie." He looked away.

Jane respected his privacy and tried to help him out by changing the subject to something he could talk on and on about. "So, is your daughter going to come up and give her approval on the new place before you make your decision?"

"Oh, land's sake, no! This day and age there ain't no reason for anyone to be put out by having to go anywhere." He fired up the engine at last and began backing out of the parking space. "I plan to scout out some lots, hook up a live video feed via my laptop and let her see what I've chosen on the spot."

"Lots?" Had she heard that right? "Not *houses*?"

"Houses? And take on somebody else's troubles? No, thank you." The mammoth vehicle lurched forward and they were on their way. "No, I want to take charge of this deal literally from the ground up. Only way to make sure it's done right and . . ."

"Cost-effectively?" Jane guessed.

"There you go! Yes. Cost-effectively. I like you, Jane. I knew I made the right choice when I asked for your help."

"Thank you." Jane sank back into the plush leather-upholstered seat. She had had her heart set on house hunting. In fact, she had been looking forward to sharing whatever history she knew about various parts of town. She had even thought about seeking out the positive selling points of the homes they would walk through and offering some tasteful decorating tips.

However, if the man wanted to look at lots, then she could adjust.

"Building a house? What an adventure!" Jane's creative mind shifted gears easily to thoughts of house plans, carpet samples, color charts for paint and tile and shutters and siding, not to mention all the landscaping to be done. "There must be some very nice lots around town that would—"

"Outside town."

"What?"

"Not *around* town. Or *in* town. I'll need a lot just outside of town to suit my building plans."

"Oh, you already have a building plan in mind?"

"In mind?" He gripped the wheel and pressed his big shoulders back, tipping his chin up and grinning. "Little lady, I already have something in transit."

"Transit? Do you mean a prefab or mobile home?"

"I mean a first-class, straight-from-a-kit, ready-to-assemble A-frame with red metal roof!"

"A-frame? Metal?" Bye-bye color charts. Bye-bye . . . "Did you say *kit*?"

"Yes, ma'am, er, Jane, yes, I did. Ordered it straight off the Internet. It will take a while before it actually gets shipped out, of course. That's why I ordered it already. Then it goes to a warehouse. After that, it can be delivered to my property within a week. Guaranteed that after the land is cleared and the foundation laid, it's just three day's work and you can hang up one of them 'Home Sweet Home' banners and move on in."

"A kit? The Internet? *Three* days?" Jane had the most unsettling sensation in the pit of her stomach. "Mr. Sturgis, if all this is so, I am not sure what you even really need me for."

"Save time."

"What? You've pared the whole process down to a matter of days. I don't see how I . . ."

"I need a contact. Someone who knows the lay of the land—figuratively *and* literally. I need someone here who can help me pick the best lot and once that's a done deal, find me a first-rate contractor to help me put it all together. Also, I will have some say-so in how things are situated inside, which way they put the fixtures and the like. And the decorating, for sure. I'll need help with that. All at the best price possible, of course."

"Of course."

"Now, I will pay you for your work. You just keep a record of your time and expenses and I will compensate you. Can you do that, Jane?"

"*It's not about what we want, Jane. It's about what God wants from us, and for us.*" Alice's words came back to her.

And Louise's: "*You never know what simple kindness or small show of support might make all the difference, Jane. Helping a stranger find a home in a new place, you have no idea which doors that might open or how the Lord might use that.*"

"Yes, Lyndon." The man needed someone to listen to him and needed a woman's touch to make the house he was building a home. He was a newcomer to Acorn Hill, and she was his contact, his neighbor. Jane sat upright and clapped her hands to show her willingness to get to work. "I don't want to be paid for being a good neighbor, but as for the rest of it, I can do that."

"Good. I hope you can do it pronto, because unless the other places that Watson fellow from the real estate office showed me are sitting on oil deposits or diamond mines, I think I've found the place for my A-frame right off the bat. Let's go walk around and see what you think. If I like it, then you grab my cell and get to finding me that contractor. Time is—"

"Money. I know." Jane couldn't help but laugh a little at the situation she had gotten herself into.

Chapter Four

Alice arrived half an hour early for her shift and headed for the nursery. She hadn't been able to get little Baby New Year out of her thoughts and couldn't wait to see what progress he had made.

Even though the holidays had passed, things at the hospital had remained slow. It was often quiet this time of year, as people tended to put off elective surgery until spring or summer. So Alice didn't think it too odd when the elevator doors leading to the maternity and nursery floor whooshed open and she faced an empty hallway. All the better to get a peek at the baby before reporting to work, she had told herself as she approached the wall-sized, well-lit window.

Just a quick peek and then . . . Alice caught her breath.

The nursery was empty.

The premature baby could not have gone home after only two days, Alice knew. What had happened?

Her pulse picked up a little as she hurried toward the nurses' station connected to the bright but silent nursery. She tried not to let her imagination and knowledge of all the things that could go wrong run away with her. She murmured a prayer that all was well.

Still, her fears must have shown in her face as she stepped into the doorway.

"He's having his first in-room visit with his mom and dad," nurse Nancy King said softly before Alice could voice her concern.

"Oh, thank goodness." Alice pressed her hand to her chest and exhaled slowly in relief. An in-room visit meant the baby had gotten stronger and did not need oxygen or constant monitoring. "No other babies born since Tuesday?"

"Nope. Seems that's the way around here. We either have a room of empty bassinets or a full house." Nancy shook her head. "You know babies, Alice. They run on God's time."

Alice looked around at this place where matters of life and death were the stuff of every day. "So do illness and accidents. That's why we always have to be prepared."

"Always ready to answer the call." Nancy gave a snappy salute.

Alice pondered Nancy's response for a moment as she stood staring into the quiet nursery, then whispered her own version of her friend's assessment. "Always ready to answer *God's* call."

"*Hmm?* What was that?" Nancy asked.

"Just . . ." Alice laughed lightly at being caught thinking out loud. "I'm just glad everything is going to be fine with our Baby New Year."

"I hope so. I pray so. Life can be so precarious, though." Usually a bright and bubbly chatterbox, today Nancy looked off into the empty nursery thoughtfully. "Especially a new life, facing struggles from the very start."

"Are you telling me that he's not out of the woods yet?"

"They think he'll be fine in time."

"In time." Alice nodded her head slowly, knowing that probably meant that he was still facing multiple health problems as many preemies do.

"We're still feeding him with a tube and monitoring blood gasses." Nancy lifted the child's chart from the rack on the wall and glanced at the information inside. "They won't let him go home until he's stable and has gained a couple of pounds."

"A couple?" Alice felt a small tremor of alarm. The child had weighed around five pounds at birth and should have gained a few ounces by now.

"He's been losing fluids. The doctor expected it."

Alice took in that information and then asked, "But the doctor also expects everything will be all right from here on out, right?

"That's what we all hope."

Hope versus expectation. In the medical world, the two could make the difference between a full recovery and . . .

"How are the parents holding up?"

Nancy paused for a moment and then raised her hand in the air, palm down, and made a wavering motion. "It varies from moment to moment. They trust that we're doing everything for their baby, and obviously, since he's getting his first in-room visit, he's doing better, but that doesn't alleviate their money concerns."

"Insurance?"

"Yes, but unfortunately there are a thousand little things, the parts not covered and the basic cost of food and shelter for the parents. Even if everything goes smoothly from now on, the docs aren't likely to release the little fellow for another two weeks, maybe not until the end of the month."

Alice winced. "What about help from outside sources?"

"From what I gather, these two young people were already expecting when they married against her parents' counsel."

"I had heard something to that effect," Alice said.

"They seem to feel that if they become a public sympathy case, it will validate their family's opinion that they are not ready and able to be parents."

"That just breaks my heart," Alice said. "Everybody needs help now and then. New life *and new marriages* need it more than most."

"The social worker did get them to agree to allow her to set up a fund within the hospital." Nancy tapped her pen against a large fishbowl with a few inches of coins on the bottom and some paper money.

Alice instinctively slipped her hand into her pocket to retrieve the small clutch of bills she kept for lunch money or the occasional treat from the vending machines. She tucked the money into the fishbowl. "I'm sure my sisters will be happy to add something too, through me, of course."

"That's so nice. You have a very special family, Alice."

The elevator dinged, letting them know someone else had arrived.

"Thank you." Alice glanced up to see a slender woman with a streak of white in her otherwise very dark hair get off on their floor. "I'm afraid they won't be able to give as much as they'd like, though, as January is a slow time at the inn."

"Really? I think it would be a lovely time of year to stay at your place." Nancy stretched her upper body to get a glimpse at the new person on the floor but kept right on talking. "I guess people have bills to pay off and tax preparations to consider and they expect the weather to be bleak—even if it's fine one day, they know it *will* change."

"Yes, and people are all traveled- and visited-out from the holidays. They just want to stay home and be quiet for a few weeks. Our business picks up in February, though."

"I bet you get a lot of couples for Valentine's Day."

"Yes, Jane is going to do a whole event this year, special meal and all. But *this* month . . . you can hardly pry some people out of their homes, no matter what."

"Tell me about it!" The dark-haired woman stood beside them, insinuating herself into their conversation with ease.

"I am having a whale of a time with speakers and workshop moderators who thought traveling in January was a great idea back in September but who suddenly are calling to cancel at an alarming rate."

Nancy shook her head in a show of empathy.

"Adding insult to injury, they use some of the flimsiest excuses you could imagine. Oh wait, what am I saying?" The stranger put her hand to her forehead. "As nurses, you could probably imagine some pretty silly excuses for people not doing what they promised they would do, am I right?"

"So right." Nancy rolled her eyes.

"I never gave it much thought, but yes, I have heard some doozies, I suppose," Alice admitted. "It comes with the territory though. You live and learn and find ways to work around their issues and objections, especially if their health is at risk."

"Yes. Right. So true." The woman, who carried a large red briefcase that dwarfed her small figure, gave Alice a broad smile. "Find a way around the issues. Yes. You do what you have to do to get the job done, am I right?"

Alice wasn't sure if that was a real or rhetorical question. Just to be polite she answered it anyway. "I never let anyone's excuses keep me from doing what's right for them, if that's what you mean."

"Bingo!" The woman snapped her fingers with a flourish and pointed one finger directly at Alice. "I like you. I like your way of looking at things. You may be just the person I need to help me wriggle out of this jam."

"Me? Jam?" Alice looked from the strange woman to her friend Nancy.

"Alice, this is Rachel Grissom. She's an event coordinator for medical . . . conventions?"

The woman, who looked to be in her early forties but exuded the energy of someone twenty years younger, swung out her hand to grasp Alice's even before Alice had offered it for shaking.

"Call me Rachel. I'm with Med/Health Career Advantage, the Service and Solutions division. We specialize in everything from providing materials for in-house in-services and seminars to offering accredited classes for continuing education and licensing for medical staff to large events such as conferences and career fairs for health-care professionals. I am so happy to meet you, Alice . . . ?"

"Howard," she said. "Alice Howard."

"Do you work on this floor?"

"No, I just came in to check on a baby before my shift starts."

"Going above and beyond the call of duty, as the saying goes?"

"All in a day's work," Alice said with a laugh as she countered with another saying.

"Didn't you just say you don't work on this floor? Pardon me for pointing this out, but that means you don't have patients here."

"It's a small hospital, Rachel. We're all concerned about the care of every patient here."

"Alice really cares about what goes on around here and that our patients get the very best treatment. She comes in early, stays late, and fills in for nurses in other units when the need arises."

"Comes in early. Fills in for others. Gives the best care. Whenever and wherever it's needed." Rachel's dark eyebrows crimped down over her questioning eyes. "Sounds like a recipe for career burnout."

"To me it's the fuel that keeps the passion for my job burning. I got into nursing to serve and care for people. I think the fastest way to burn out is to deny that part of ourselves and begin to look at patients only in terms of charts and orders. They are much more, and if we keep sight of that, we become more than someone just doing a job."

"You do this kind of thing often? This coming in early to check on patients?"

Nancy stood up and gestured broadly, placing her hands, with nails neatly manicured with pink sparkling polish to match her pink and lavender scrubs, on Alice's shoulder. "Alice practically holds this hospital together."

"Oh no. That's not . . ." Alice held up her hands and took a step back, as if to distance herself from such a bold statement. "That's overstating things quite a bit."

"Okay, the Alices of the world hold hospitals like ours together," Nancy conceded with a sweet crinkle of her nose and a twinkle in her eye that rivaled the glitter on her nails. "She's tireless."

Alice raised one thick-soled shoe and wiggled her foot. "Tell that to my feet at the end of a shift."

"Always cheerful," Nancy said.

"My sisters might argue with that," Alice joked.

"Pitches in without complaining and makes real connections with the staff as well as with the patients and their families."

"I try."

"I can only speak for myself but when I see Alice in the hallway, I get a little more spring in my step because I know things are going to go a little more smoothly around here because of her."

"That's so sweet, Nancy, but I think the same could be said of you and most of the staff here," Alice protested.

"Oh, I don't know. This is a wonderful hospital, but even the best workplace has its standouts." Rachel said. "Alice, you may just be the person I am looking for."

"For what?" Alice didn't know whether to feel flattered or apprehensive.

"I told you. I've had a whole raft of cancellations for my latest conference. We need speakers, and I think you would make a very positive impression on the audience."

"No. No, if you put me up in front of an entire conference of people I don't think I'd make a very good impression at all." She put her cool palm against her suddenly warm cheek. "Oh no. No thank you. It's not for me."

"Look, it wouldn't have to be the entire conference." Rachel reached into her red briefcase and began fishing around for something, without breaking the rapid rate of her animated speech. "The closest you would come to that would be if you were part of the panel discussion at the conclusion of the event on Saturday."

"On Saturday?"

Rachel went right on searching without answering Alice or even looking up at her. If she *had* looked up she would have seen a woman with a deer-in-headlights expression.

"Even the large gathering at the end of the conference will probably have only half of the participants in the audience. Attendance tends to drop off, you know, as the day wears on."

"Half?" *Of a medical conference?* That still seemed like an awful lot of people.

"But you do not have to sign on for the closing panel, though you would be perfect for it." Finally she produced what she had been searching for—a five-by-seven-inch leather binder. "I also have openings scattered all through the two-day event."

"Two days?"

"Friday and Saturday."

"This coming Friday and Saturday?"

"No, no. The twenty-third and the twenty-fourth." She tapped the dates on a calendar with her French-manicured nail. "That would give you three weeks to prepare."

"Alice is always prepared," Nancy teased, using Alice's own words. "You should do this, Alice. It would be fun. I bet it's even in an exotic locale."

"Philadelphia," Rachel said in a brusque monotone.

"Oh." Nancy sighed, practically pouting as she repeated, "Philadelphia."

"That's why I am visiting hospitals within driving distance to recruit my fill-in speakers. With such short notice, I am really scrambling for people who might be able to fill the slots without too much inconvenience."

"I went to nursing school in Philadelphia." Actually that part made the idea more intriguing to Alice. "I have friends there."

"You could go a day early and stay through Sunday. All at a lovely hotel and on our tab."

"You mean I wouldn't have to pay?"

"Pay? No, Alice, we'd pay you." She scribbled a number down on the back of her business card and handed it to Alice. "Yes, we pay our speakers quite well. In fact, some professionals leave the medical field and take on presenting programs for their livelihood."

Alice couldn't imagine such a thing. Leave medicine and helping people in order to talk about medicine to the people in the trenches who were doing the real helping?

"We provide the cost of lodging, as I said, a speaking fee, plus a stipend to cover expenses. Or if you'd like to stay with your friends, we could give you a bump in your fee instead. It's not a large amount but enough to pay for taxis, tips and three meals if you aren't extravagant."

"Or one really nice meal if you are. Extravagant, that is. Only Alice isn't." Nancy raised her shoulders and lowered them again. "I only wish *I* could do it, but I never could organize my thoughts well enough to share them with an audience."

Rachel jotted down the amount that would be given for meals just below the payment amount on the business card.

Alice's gaze moved from the generous amount Rachel had listed to the fishbowl with the few bills that she had dropped on top. Alice could put the speaking fee to good use for the new baby and his parents. "Are you sure that you don't want to do it, Nancy?"

"Oh, you know me." Nancy shrugged. "I can talk and talk and talk and talk, but too much of the time, I never get around to really saying anything." Nancy laughed. "Besides, I've jumped from job to job, place to place, and left nursing altogether to raise my kids. No, I'm in no position to teach anyone, not like you, Alice. Besides, I don't want to spend two days in Philadelphia, but you know some people there."

Alice thought of Virginia Herman. She and Virginia had been friends for years. It would be good to go and spend time with her. And with Mark.

Mark Graves and Alice had dated in college, but then the relationship could not overcome his lack of a committed and vital faith. When they found each other again not so long ago, Mark had discovered his faith. But they had changed. While they still cared for each other and enjoyed each other's company, they were not ready to be more than really good friends. Maybe some day their relationship would grow into something different, but for now . . .

The phones ringing at the nurses' station jarred Alice out of her reverie.

Nancy answered and launched into a series of quick responses. "Uh-huh. Sure. Nope. Yep. Absolutely." Then she laughed lightly and said, "That's what we're here for. We'll be ready."

Rachel waited quietly during the one-sided conversation, and the instant it was over, she raised her pen as if ready to jot down something and asked, "So, what do you think about the conference, Alice?"

"It seems like a terrific opportunity, Rachel—"

"Sorry to have to cut things short, Kelly," Nancy spoke into the intercom.

Alice waited for Nancy to finish speaking before completing her response to Rachel.

"We have a new mama coming up, and she's so far along they're afraid she might deliver in the elevator. So we have to get our little baby back in the nursery and everything in order to keep things on track." Nancy lifted her finger off the intercom button long enough for Kelly, the nurse's aide, to reply that she and the baby would be there in a moment.

"I guess it's about to get pretty busy around here." Rachel glanced upward at the clock on the wall behind Nancy.

Alice did the same. "Oh dear. I need to get moving. I have only ten minutes until my shift starts."

It wouldn't take her ten minutes to get to her station, but she did like to be on the floor ahead of time. Also, having to rush off to the job she loved made a very handy excuse for not lingering and talking to Rachel about the job she didn't know if she really wanted to take on.

"Alice, before you go, I can give you some more details on the conference. Why don't you look them over and get back to me by the end of the day?" Rachel opened her briefcase again.

"No. That won't be necessary." Alice held up her hand and took a step toward the elevator.

Rachel stopped searching and met Alice's gaze, her eyes practically sparkling with hope for good news. "Oh, so you've made up your mind already?"

"I'm going to have to ask you ladies to move away from the nursery now. Our little Baby New Year is coming on through." Nancy pointed to a small commotion approaching in the hallway.

Alice gently took Rachel by the arm and led her away. They stood against the wall by the elevator and watched as the nurse's aide rolled along the portable crib. Inside, a very small bundle squirmed and made the tiniest little *mmm*'s and gasps and gurgles.

Alice held her breath. Squirming was good. *Mmm*'s and gurgles were good. The gasps? Alice wasn't so sure.

The wary, anxious expressions on the faces of the clearly exhausted parents did nothing to reassure her.

"That's such a tiny baby," Rachel whispered.

"And the parents are hardly any more than kids themselves," Alice observed. This was the first time she'd actually laid eyes on the pair. She looked from their faces to the fishbowl. Suddenly her lunch money seemed a pretty pitiful offering. She dropped her gaze to the business card in her hand and the amount she stood to earn if she would only accept the call to duty.

"Bring that baby on in here," Nancy called to the aide. "Mama and Daddy, you come on in too. You can sit here in the nursery with your sweet one as long as you want, but we need to get settled because we have another new arrival on the way."

Ding.

The elevator clunked to a stop a few feet farther down the hall.

Nancy beamed at Alice. "What did I tell you?"

"Babies run on God's time, so we always have to be ready to answer God's call," Alice said softly, giving Nancy a wave.

"Alice?" Rachel tapped her on the shoulder. "You never answered my question. Have you made up your mind about the conference?"

"Yes, I have." Alice stole one last glance at Baby New Year and his young parents and at the fishbowl offering that would hardly make a dent in the bills they were running up. Then she turned and smiled at the event planner. "Yes. I have made up my mind. You can put me on your schedule. I'll do it."

Chapter Five

Wednesday evening the sisters gathered around the kitchen table and said grace over heaping bowls of Jane's rendition of Texas-style chili.

"I guess you can't spend the day with a man in a cowboy hat extolling the virtues of all things Texan without having it show up in some other aspect of your life," Louise observed. She placed her napkin in her lap and inhaled to savor the delicious aroma of meat, tomato sauce and spices.

"I hope you like it." Jane got up to get something from the counter. "Lyndon and I finally agreed that he would pay me by buying my meals when we're working together and then, when he couldn't find any of what he called 'real' chili in town, he offered me pickled eggs and hot links from jars in the tiny refrigerator in his SUV."

"I'm surprised you have the stomach for chili tonight then," Alice teased.

"I respectfully declined the eggs and links, thank you very much." She set down a tray with two kinds of crackers arranged in an attractive spiral pattern on it. "But I've had a craving for that chili he talked about ever since."

"Do we have more of that wonderful corn bread?" Alice asked.

"Sorry, I didn't even think about making some. I do have some excellent grated cheese to sprinkle on top of the chili. It's Amish smoky sharp cheddar." Jane whisked away the lid on a ceramic dish filled with finely shredded cheese that added a new and tempting aroma to the air. "And in the other dish, some homemade sour cream."

"Homemade? I had no idea you knew how to do that." Louise was always surprised by her sister's culinary abilities.

"Just wait until you taste it. You'll be so spoiled you'll never want to have the stuff from a plastic container again," Jane lifted the second container and dipped up a dollop for Louise.

Alice raised a spoonful of the rich mix of chili, cheese and sour cream and took a taste. "*Mmm.*"

"Oh, and there are dark chocolate brownies for dessert." Jane pointed to the oven. "You can thank Lyndon for that suggestion too. Apparently there is some connection between chocolate and chili. In fact, some cooks he knows use cocoa as an ingredient in their chili."

"You can't keep cooking these Southern dishes, Jane," Alice protested.

"Why not?" Jane stopped crumbling crackers into her bowl. "I thought you liked them."

"I do! I do! I like them too much. If I keep eating like this, I won't be able to squeeze into my best suit when I go to that conference in Philadelphia near the end of the month."

The sisters laughed.

"I am so impressed that you have decided to do that," Louise said. "You have so much to share."

"I know I brought it up, but if you don't mind, I'd rather not talk about the conference just yet. I've had a busy day and I am very tired. If I think too much about getting up and talking in front of a crowd of people, I won't be able to settle down tonight and get any rest."

"I know what you mean. When I was young, I used to allow myself to get keyed up before my concerts. That was a recipe for a restless night." Louise turned her attention to Jane. "So, beyond his questionable culinary offerings, how did you get along with Lyndon today?"

"Like everything in life, the day had its ups and downs." She sprinkled some more of the soft curls of cheese over the thick, meaty mix in her bowl. "On the up side, after talking to every contractor in the area, he admitted that Clark Barrett, my original recommendation, was really the best of the bunch."

"He won't be sorry with that choice," Louise agreed.

"No. It peeved him that none of the contractors, including Clark, was willing to drop everything and start work on his project instantly. But when he considered how easygoing and flexible Clark could be, as well as his being right here in town, Lyndon calmed down."

"Calmed down?" Alice searched Jane's face in concern. "He doesn't have a bad temper, does he?"

"Oh, not really. He gets agitated but never aggressive," Jane explained. "Once I realized he just wanted a friend in his new part-time hometown and saw how much he is still grieving for his wife, I was able to overlook his eccentricities."

"Good."

"However . . ." Jane chewed at her lower lip.

"Yes?" Louise asked.

Jane sighed. "His lack of patience concerns me. He rushes here and there, trying to save a few cents and not using *common sense* sometimes. I mean, I offer ideas and, before I can even flesh them out for his consideration, he rejects them and moves on."

"A lot of men are like that," Louise said. "They know what they want, and that's all there is to it."

"That's his right, of course, as the home owner. My

concern is that he asks me about something, which suggests that he doesn't know what he wants, and then he is in such a hurry he doesn't fully listen to my response and rushes on to the next stage."

"That would be frustrating." Alice took a cracker from the tray.

"It's not so much frustrating as it is worrying. I think that his behavior is going to come back to haunt him at some point in this process."

"But he did take your advice about Clark."

"After he called a whole list of others, checking prices and seeing who could be available the quickest," Jane reminded them. "I wonder if he's using this project to avoid dealing with how much he misses his wife."

"That is entirely possible. And it does sound as if the project could go wrong along the way, if he isn't honest with himself about his feelings." Louise folded her hands in her lap and studied Jane for a moment before saying, "I intend to keep you and Mr. Sturgis and this whole project in my prayers until it's finished."

"Thanks, Louise. I appreciate that. Maybe I am just reading too much into his behavior. The project will probably be fine."

"True, not every snap decision is a recipe for disaster, of course." Alice said, her expression thoughtful.

"You are fretting about your own decision, thinking you may have acted rashly, aren't you?" Louise knew her sister so well.

"Yes, I am."

"Oh, Alice, think of all the fun you'll have," Jane said, encouraging her older sister.

"Fun? As a speaker on a panel?"

"That's only one part of it. You'll also get to mingle with other professionals. And you'll see your friend Virginia and get a chance to spend time with Mark," Jane held up her fingers as she counted off all the positive things Alice had to look forward to. "You can go sightseeing and shopping and—"

"You make it sound so good that I wish I were going with her." Louise laughed.

"Would you?" Alice asked.

Louise shook her head. "You know I'd love to, but I have my responsibilities to my students. We just started learning pieces for the spring recital this week."

"Recital pieces." Alice nodded. "Since I'm going to be part of a question-and-answer panel, I only have to come up with a few words about keeping a fresh outlook about work. At least I don't have to memorize something and get it right, note for note."

"There's something positive to think about right there," Jane pointed out.

"I'll try to remember that." Alice gave Louise an anxious glance. "Now, let's put aside that topic until the morning, shall we?"

"Let's," Louise agreed. "We'll need something interesting to discuss as we finally tackle putting away those Christmas boxes tomorrow."

As they brought the boxes down into the basement Thursday morning, Louise asked Alice if she had been able to get a good night's rest.

"For the most part, but then I had one of those dreams where you find yourself in school about to take a test you haven't prepared for." Alice laughed. "Isn't the human mind a funny thing?"

"I'd say it's a remarkable thing," Louise observed. "Dreams are often our way of dealing with our anxieties in a safe environment."

"There's no need to be anxious, Alice," Jane chimed in.

"You said you'd do it, you'll do the prep work and you'll be great."

"It made perfect sense at the time that I committed to do it," Alice said as the sisters neatly tucked away boxes of Christmas decorations on a shelf in the basement. "But in the cold light of a new day . . ."

"Alice? The last box?" Louise pointed, indicating the box Alice had carried downstairs.

Alice looked down, her expression still a bit unfocused. "What about it?"

"Heave ho, let's go!" Jane reached down and hoisted up the lightweight box, supporting it with one knee so that Louise could take hold of it and push it into place on the shelf in front of them. "If I didn't know you better, Alice, I'd think you were trying to get out of doing your part."

"Oh no . . . I would never . . ."

"We know," Jane said laughing and slipped her arm around her older sister, dropping the kid sister tone. "I'm just making a bad joke. We know you always do your share and then some."

"Thank you, Jane. I certainly hope that I do."

"Tea, anyone?" Louise rubbed her hands together. "I'm making it."

"Lovely!" Jane gave Louise's shoulders a squeeze.

"Perfect." Alice pushed at a corner of a container to line it up straight and nodded. "I get a chill in my bones when I'm down here more than a few minutes."

Alice brushed away a smudge of dust from her pale, comfy-looking jeans. "As I was saying about this sudden decision to take on conference speaking, it seemed the right thing to do. If you had seen how little money we had collected, if you knew what bills that young couple may face, or if you had gotten a look at their anxious faces, you each would have done the same thing."

"Not me," Ethel called down from where she waited at

the top of the stairs. This morning she had excused herself from the box detail as "not dressed for heavy lifting." However, she had generously offered to stand by the door and be ready to answer the phone or the door or to do whatnot while they finished their chore. She also had the perfect vantage point to listen in on their conversation and call down her opinions.

"Faced with the same offer to go off to another city and step in for somebody who obviously didn't want the job in the first place, I most certainly would not have volunteered. Now I can see Louise or Jane doing that, but I'd never have guessed that you, Alice, my little shrinking violet, would step up."

"Shrinking violet?" Alice paused, and then she moved her gaze toward her sisters. "Is that what I am, a shrinking violet?"

"Violets are beautiful," Jane said cheerily.

"Alice is not a shrinking violet. There is nothing wrong with not wanting the limelight," said Louise. "That's why she makes such a wonderful nurse. She deals with patients and doctors and all sorts of unexpected situations all the time and never makes the problems about herself. Even this commitment—it isn't about what she wants but about what she needed to do to help those parents and their new baby."

"That is so true." Jane drew her arm away from Louise's shoulder to reach out and pat Alice on the back. "That's just Aunt Ethel's way of saying what went through all our minds when you announced that you had committed yourself to speaking in front of a large group. 'That's not like Alice.'"

"It won't be a *large* group." Alice corrected softly, hopefully.

"Don't fret over it." Louise headed for the stairs. "You'll do fine, and you'll get in a nice visit with Mark and Virginia in the bargain."

"That was no small factor," Alice admitted. "As I get older, I value those ties more and more."

"I too." Louise put her foot on the first step and looked up to Ethel in the well-lit doorway. "I have been so blessed throughout my life by so many people who helped, guided, taught and, most of all, loved me. Aunt Ethel and I were just talking about the number of people we've known and how, sadly, it's possible that we've forgotten some of them."

In that instant something, or rather some*one*, who had been on her mind popped in again. She paused with her hand on the rail and turned to Alice. "In fact, there's someone in Philadelphia I'd like you to check in on when you get there."

"Certainly. Who?"

"Do you remember my old neighbor, Agnes Pennington?"

"Of course." Alice turned to Jane, "I met her when Louise was first married and I was in nursing school. She was this darling, spry woman who lived next door to Louise and Eliot in a grand old Victorian house that had been in her family for generations. She and her husband had the sweetest relationship. You could tell that she adored him and he just doted on her."

"They had their disagreements, believe me." Louise had her ear bent a time or two by Mrs. Pennington when the pair had a squabble. "But they had the dearest way of making up. After they cooled down and worked things out, they wrote each other love letters and left them where the other partner would find them."

"*Aah.*" Jane's expression went a bit wistful.

"I confess I sometimes envied her, having those endearing messages to read again and again to remind her of him after he died a few years back."

As Louise went up the stairs, she continued talking. "Her door was always open to young couples just starting out. Sometimes I even took advantage of that when I needed a sounding board, another woman who could offer guidance or just lend an ear. Mrs. Pennington always had solid advice on marriage and, later, on parenting."

"I'll be happy to check in on her," Alice said as she walked upstairs behind Louise.

"Good." Louise reached the kitchen. "We haven't kept in touch as much as I'd have liked over the last few years but we have always exchanged letters at Christmastime. But this year, I received nothing at all from her. Not even a card."

"Have you tried calling her?" Jane followed her sisters into the kitchen.

"I will before Alice gets there, but my fear is that over the phone she will simply say everything is all right and not to worry. Unless someone sees her and talks to her in person, I would still worry that something is wrong."

"How old is she?" Ethel asked.

"She is easily into her eighties by now and living alone in a big house."

"In her eighties?" Ethel fluffed up the back of her vivid red hair. "My, that *is* old to live on one's own."

The sisters exchanged loving but knowing smiles.

"I worry that she may be ill or infirm and have no one to turn to. She helped me get a good start in my adult life. I want to make sure she isn't forgotten."

Alice and Ethel sat at the kitchen table while Jane went to fill the teakettle and Louise got a tin of tea from the pantry.

"That is just as it should be, Louise," Ethel said with a nod. "You should look after this poor old dear. People just don't do that anymore."

"Look out for one another?" Alice asked.

"Give their elders their due," Ethel told her. "So many young people fail to turn to older people who have been down life's twisting paths to get guidance and support." Ethel shook her head and sighed. "That's exactly why I voted my approval for Patsy Ley to go ahead with her experiment."

That nonsequitur stopped Jane and Louise cold, but

Alice concurred with her aunt. "Yes. It's worth exploring, though I don't know how the church can afford that kind of undertaking without charging participants or cutting back somewhere else."

"It's just a trial," Ethel said. "No use putting the horse before the cart."

Louise gave Jane a warning look before suggesting sweetly, "Don't you mean putting the cart before the horse, Aunt Ethel?"

"Horse. Cart. Cart. Horse. We'll all know more after this afternoon's meeting."

"Who'll be attending the meeting, Aunt Ethel?" Alice asked.

"Just the McGuffeys and Henry and Patsy, of course. It's her baby, really."

"Baby?" Jane sat down, her eyes wide.

Louise understood her surprise. Henry Ley, the Associate Pastor at Grace Chapel, and his wife Patsy had no children and appeared too mature to start a family now.

"I don't suppose the two of you could enlighten those of us not on the board about what you are discussing?" Louise said "the *two* of you" but she had fixed her gaze squarely on Alice.

"Enlighten you? Louise, dear, haven't you been listening? It's what we've been talking about all this time. Older people. Life's twisting paths. Your former neighbor," Ethel said, as if the string of words would prompt Louise into instant understanding.

"Making Marriage Matter." Alice tapped her finger on the kitchen table to accentuate each word. "It's a program that Patsy learned about from another church's newsletter."

"You know how wild she is about weddings and young couples," Ethel interjected.

Louise put the tea tray on the table. "What kind of program?"

"Well, that's just it. It's only in the idea phase now. Patsy, with Henry's input, of course, has gathered all sorts of materials on building strong marriages. They would like to start a new effort in the church to offer an outreach to our younger married couples."

"You know young people today." Ethel rolled her eyes heavenward and shook her head but did not elaborate further.

"They want to match newer-marrieds with long-time couples as a sort of mentoring set-up." Alice laced her fingers together to illustrate forming a connection. "To listen, teach and, mostly, lead by example.

"As Mrs. Pennington and her husband did." Louise poured boiling water over the tea in the teapot. She put her shoulders back and could feel her very spirit lifting at the thought of how much good a project like that might do. "I like the idea. I like it very much."

"Nothing is set in stone yet. Patsy has gathered the names of our handful of newlyweds and has asked Mac and Maggie McGuffey to serve as our trial mentors."

"The McGuffeys." Louise did not know them well, but they always treated each other with love and respect, and everyone in the church knew they could turn to the couple if they ever needed anything. "That's a fine choice."

"They are meeting this afternoon to discuss which couple would make the best match, and to decide how they will proceed."

"So, I guess it's all set then?" Louise asked.

"No. It's all unset." Alice broke her hands apart and laughed lightly. "That's why they are meeting. The idea is to form a whole network around the young couples, so they'd like more involvement but people are so busy these days."

"I'm not," Louise said softly. Was this it? Was this her call to duty?

"What?" Alice asked.

"I'm not that busy, really. I have my students, yes. But

otherwise the inn will be fairly quiet until things start to pick up in February. I have time to lend to the project, and having been one who benefited from this exact kind of thing, I would love the chance to give back in kind."

"I have to hand it to Lyndon Sturgis," Jane said as she went to the pantry to retrieve a container of homemade biscotti she had stored there.

Louise poured the tea as she asked, "What do you mean about Mr. Sturgis?"

"I admire him for wanting to remain close and available to his daughter and her new baby."

"Ah." Louise sat down. "I heard you take a call from him this morning. Any new developments?"

"He put in an offer on the lot."

"Just like that?" Alice snapped her fingers.

"Just like that," Jane confirmed, snapping her fingers as well. "He has to wait to see if the offer is accepted. Knowing him and his need to get the best of every price negotiation, it might take a little back and forth before it's settled. Then there will be some lag time as all the legalities are tended to."

"Will he be heading back to Texas then?" Louise asked.

"No. He probably will go for a short visit when he's got things lined up but can't start work on the house. He's staying with his son-in-law's family in Merriville until then."

"He accepts your time and help for free but won't even pay for a room here at the inn?" Ethel sniffed.

"He offered to pay me. I was the one who refused him. I don't mind about his not staying here, really," Jane said. "There is such a thing as too much togetherness."

"Yes, I guess I can see what you mean," Ethel agreed.

"If all goes smoothly, he will have the deed on the land in the next week to ten days. Then he has to prepare the land, and then the kit will arrive and that will be that."

"In a week?" Alice frowned.

"He'll have the lot quickly since it's a private, cash sale," Jane said. "So, as long as this mild weather lasts and he can get all the prep work done, he should have the basic house up and be doing the finish work by the end of the month."

"Really? That fast? What a learning experience this project must be for you," Louise said.

"If you mean learning how to deal with someone who always has a gadget in his hand and an issue on his mind that he expects me to handle, then, yes, I'd say so." Jane laughed.

"I felt bad giving him over to Clark Barrett to order supplies this morning. I just hope Lyndon listens and doesn't make it more difficult for Clark to do his job. Lyndon Sturgis is a man who wants everything done yesterday."

"Sturgis?" Ethel cocked her head to one side. "That's the fellow who made his wife carry used tea bags around in her purse, isn't it? Jane, dear, what have you gotten yourself into?"

"It's not so bad, really. Yes, he's picky and a penny-pincher, but deep down I think he's a big softie with a penchant for good stewardship."

"Good stewardship over tea bags, maybe, but I don't know how that relates to real life," Ethel clearly remained unconvinced. "Let me tell you, Jane, about people who mistake stinginess for good stewardship. They often cost themselves, and the folks who have to deal with them, more time, frustration and money than they save."

"Lyndon says time *is* money."

"*Tsk, tsk*," Ethel chided, shaking her head.

"I told him what Benjamin Franklin said about time being the stuff of life, but I don't think it made much of an impression." Jane accepted more tea from Louise. "Anyway, I plan to follow up at the site as often as I can. I'll probably go see what I can do to help move things along tomorrow as well. Anyway, I'm in for the long haul now. I can't wait to see how it all comes together. I feel as though I can actually accomplish something if I just hang with it and do what needs doing."

"Good luck with that," Louise said, lifting her tea cup in salute. "Here's to reporting for duty."

"Speaking of reporting," Alice said, stealing a peek at her watch, "that first meeting is at one o'clock, Louise."

"One?" Louise set down her cup with a clink. "Will you take care of the dishes, Jane?"

"Sure."

"I have to call Patsy and Henry and volunteer my services for their project. I'm not really sure what they need at this point, but maybe, since they haven't gotten it all worked out, they can use another set of willing hands."

Chapter Six

"Here they are," Patsy Ley said as she carried a stack of colored files into Henry's airy home office.

Even though Henry was the associate pastor, the Leys occupied Grace Chapel's recently refurbished rectory. They had taken up residence there when their rental home had been destroyed in a storm. Rev. Thompson, a widower, preferred to live simply and was happy to take an apartment over the Acorn Hill Antique Shop so that the Leys could live in the rectory.

In exchange, Henry and Patsy often made their home available for church business, especially informal meetings and private teaching or counseling sessions. The office had a bank of windows along one wall and floor-to-ceiling built-in bookshelves on the opposite wall. It was the ideal gathering place for small groups.

The ivory and pale green decor gave the room a calming atmosphere. A desk sat in front of the bookshelves, and six upholstered chairs fit neatly around an antique harvest table at one end of the room. The ambiance was welcoming, but not to the degree of giving one the feeling of intruding on a private home setting.

Henry sat at the head of the table. Louise had taken the seat on Henry's right. Patsy plopped down the folders in front of the place next to Louise.

"Everything we need to know about our candidates is right here," she declared. "Now all we have to do is to make the best selection." She smiled brightly at Louise, her hands folded in front of her fuzzy pink sweater. "We'll go through those as soon as the McGuffeys arrive."

Louise checked the time, and then sat back in the cushioned chair. "Fine. I look forward to getting involved in this project and helping to develop it."

"I am so glad you decided to participate, Louise." Patsy moved behind her husband, putting her hands on his shoulders.

The Leys had a sweet ease between them that reassured Louise that no one else could have headed the Making Marriage Matter project as well as they.

"Can I get you anything to drink, Louise? Tea? Coffee?" Patsy asked.

"Thank you but no. I just had a cup of tea with my aunt and sisters."

"Ah, tea with the ladies. How cozy." She leaned to one side to address Henry, "Maybe we should have teas at the church one Friday a month."

"One new project at a time, p-please," Henry smiled as he looked at his wife over the top of his glasses.

"Sorry. You know me. Everything sounds so interesting I have a hard time staying focused." Patsy gave a quiet giggle. "It's just that one thing leads to another and then another. Henry says my train of thought doesn't need much to jump the track."

Louise laughed, and then said to Patsy and Henry, "While we're waiting for the others, I would love to hear more about the Making Marriage Matter concept."

"Louise, you will just—" Patsy launched in speaking.

"It all st-st-started—" Henry said.

"Oh." Patsy pulled out her chair and perched on the edge of the seat. "You tell about it, sweetheart."

"I think maybe you have a b-better grasp," he deferred to his wife.

Henry Ley, a short man with white hair and glasses, always looked neat and totally pulled together. Louise's father, and after him the Rev. Thompson, had relied on Henry for many things at Grace Chapel, but not for preaching or other public-speaking duties. Though his difficulty did not hamper person-to-person communication, Henry had struggled for most of his life with stuttering.

Louise sat forward, uncapping her pen in order to take notes and jot down any questions she might want to pose later.

"Well, okay." Patsy straightened her back and took a moment to gather her thoughts. "I read an article about the divorce rate that linked it to, among other things, how many young people come from homes already touched by divorce. Another factor was the way we live now—everyone so busy, people constantly on the move, families not remaining in proximity. So many young couples only have other young people to talk to about their concerns."

Louise wrote notes as Patsy talked.

"Often the people they *do* try to discuss their problems with either don't have the skills or are coping with similar problems or, worst of all, don't place great importance on holding a marriage together."

"I wish I could say I find all this surprising." Louise shook her head.

"Yes. I know what you mean. Because of these factors, it's easier for people to give up on their vows and spouses with a shrug and a sigh, thinking, 'I'll have better luck next time.'"

"I want to believe this is not the kind of thing we see in our young people at Grace Chapel or in Acorn Hill for that matter," Louise said.

"I'd like to b-believe that too." Henry passed a magazine

article to Louise. "These are s-some statistics from a period-ical for m-ministers. When young couples split, it sends rip-ples throughout the church, even the community at large."

Louise looked over the numbers.

"Even if this is not p-prevalent at Grace Chapel, it is a reality of our world. As elder members of our church, it is our responsibility to take p-proactive measures. Too often the church model is to respond after p-problems arise and divide couples."

"Then we move in to comfort and try to help heal." Patsy touched the edge of one of the articles with her fingertips to tilt the page so she could look it over herself. "That is an important mission, without question, but wouldn't it be bet-ter for the church to try to keep it from happening in the first place?"

"I suppose one regards faith in and of itself as a proactive measure. Fortification against the pitfalls and problems of the world." Louise slid back the paper in front of her to the pastor. "If only it worked that way unfailingly."

Henry nodded.

"Well, since it doesn't, we have to dedicate ourselves to standing in the gap between practicing unwavering faith and living in a fallen world." Patsy spread her hands far apart.

"I'd like to think most of us are a little c-closer than that." Henry held his own hands closer together.

"This program sounds very worthwhile, but how do you plan to go about it?" Louise asked.

"I did a lot of research and selected materials from three different churches that have taken on a similar obligation." Patsy thumbed through the files at her side. "I can give you those after this meeting, if you like."

Louise made a note not to leave without that information.

"We thought if we could match our mentor couple to a couple we feel could b-b-benefit from the experience and get them together over the course of, say, a weekend, we could try a b-bit of all three methodologies. That way we can find the right one for us."

Louise nodded. "Very well thought out . . . and exciting as well." She liked that they had taken a studied approach. That they wanted to build a curriculum and tailor it to the needs of Grace Chapel's congregants spoke to her own way of dealing with such a large undertaking. "You seem to have thought of everything."

Henry and Patsy exchanged glances.

"No?" Louise looked from one of them to the other.

"Well, as I said, ideally we would try to compress this experiment—"

"Trial run," Henry corrected.

"This *trial run* for our worthy endeavor," Patsy inserted his suggestion and kept speaking without missing a beat, "should rightly span as short a time as possible with the couples spending as much time together as is practical."

"That makes sense."

"Maggie McGuffey volunteered her home for a weekend, but that would come with a whole set of built-in . . . disruptions."

"TV, phone, reminders of waiting workloads," Louise supplied, listing all the things people came to the inn to escape.

"Among other things. Also, if you know Maggie, you know she would feel obligated to act as hostess. She'd actually delight in it, but that would detract from her role as mentor."

"I see the dilemma." Louise had a possible solution to the problem, but she didn't want to make the offer until she had a better idea what the undertaking might entail. "How soon would you like to have this trial run?"

"We hope to have a big launch around Valentine's Day, so sometime prior to that," Patsy said.

"That soon?"

"Well, it's all flexible."

"It's all conditional," Henry chimed in just a few seconds behind his wife, "on if we all agree that the program is feasible and a productive use of church resources."

"That's his way of saying, if it doesn't look like it will cost too much."

"How much cost would be involved?"

"Well, there will be study materials and then, if we begin each match-up with a weekend getaway, well, the church should take on some of the burden of that since we don't want to exclude anyone based on an inability to afford a weekend away."

"Indeed." Louise took a deep breath and held it to keep from blurting out the obvious solution. She could offer the use of the inn for the trial weekend. However, she wanted to talk to her sisters first. They would agree, she knew, especially if they picked a weekend when the inn would not otherwise be booked.

"Ding-dong! I know we're late. Take it up with Mac. I couldn't pry him out of his routine." Maggie McGuffey came sweeping into the room, removing her jacket with one hand while holding a platter of cookies in the other.

Barely five-feet tall, the energetic blonde filled any room she entered with her sweetness and joy. And the woman hardly ever visited without an offering of homemade cookies, brownies, cake or some other delectable treat. She often joked that when she retired from her work as an insurance agent everyone in town would gain ten pounds each from all the baked goods she'd make full time. She talked of starting a business baking wedding cakes. To which her husband of thirty-four years, G. W. "Mac" McGuffey, would often chime in, "And if she ever misplaces the tiny bride for the top of a wedding cake, she can hop up and stand there herself."

This afternoon Mac was strolling along behind his wife, not looking his jovial self. "You'll have to pardon me for being a bit out of sorts. I've taken Friday afternoons off for years and have a sort of pattern. That means a long lunch, a short nap. Then I'm ready for anything."

"We do appreciate your b-breaking with that routine today, Mac." Henry stood and held out his hand.

Mac shook it and gave Louise a polite, if a bit groggy, nod of greeting. After taking his wife's jacket and laying it across the back of an empty chair, he took a seat.

"Routine." Maggie settled the plate of cookies on the table and whisked away the cling-wrap covering to unleash the aroma of still warm chocolate chips. She turned to her husband and teased, "That's pastor-talk for rut."

"N-no." Alarm shone in Henry Ley's eyes and his stuttering worsened, as it sometimes did in stressful situations. "I n-n-never said—"

"I'm just needling Mac a little, Henry." Maggie held up her hand to indicate she meant nothing by the remark. She smiled and, in doing so, showed off the dimples that charmed everyone she met. "Just my way of reminding my fifty-two-year-old husband that maybe only for today he can get by without his nap."

"I d-don't know that I can take s-sides on that issue, Maggie. I confess to having s-stolen a few after-lunch w-winks from time to time myself." Henry chuckled softly.

"Hey, I like what I like. My habits have served me just fine so far." Mac sat back in the chair, relaxing at last as his contented demeanor returned and he grinned. "All I'm saying is, why mess with perfection?"

Maggie laughed and gave her husband a peck on the cheek before she sat down at the table at last. "Okeydokey, let's get started. If we act quickly enough, maybe the men can still sneak in a light snooze before dinner."

Patsy agreed with a laugh. Then she took her seat and, after a brief recap of the Making Marriage Matter concept, dived into the reason for their coming together. "We have three possible candidate couples for the trial weekend."

"This is so exciting. I feel like a beauty pageant judge waiting to see who made the final round." Maggie pushed her chair in close and planted her elbows on the tabletop.

Patsy withdrew a file from her pile and put it down on the table. "The Faradays. Aren't they just darling?"

"T-they are good kids," Henry agreed.

"Indeed." Louise had known the young man and woman since they were in diapers. "But are they really what you had in mind, Henry, for the kind of couple who would benefit from a marriage mentoring program?"

Henry narrowed his eyes. "Actually, Louise, they are exactly what I had in mind."

A single raised eyebrow was the only sign Louise gave of her surprise at that statement.

"Let me clarify. Jack and Jill Faraday could be the p-poster couple for what I had in mind in forming a support network for fledgling marriages."

"Well, they have it all, don't they?" Patsy flipped open the file in front of her to reveal a three-page, fully filled-out questionnaire. "Both were raised in the church. They had an extended courtship that endured the separation of Jack's going to school in Chicago and Jill's attending college in Philadelphia.

"And after college, they returned to Acorn Hill, took jobs, worked a year to save some money and then married last spring." Patsy closed the file and pushed it to the center of the table for anyone else to peruse.

"That's why I wouldn't have thought they'd make the best test couple," Louise said. "They have friends and all of their family living close by, lending support."

"Sometimes family so close can bring its own challenges to a marriage." Mac spoke up.

Maggie laughed. "He wanted to spend New Year's Eve at home watching TV and going to bed early, but then my sister spotted our lights on and our car in the drive after she dropped off her daughter at a slumber party and the next thing you know—"

"It's midnight, way past my bedtime and my house is filled with relatives blowing noisemakers and singing," Mac finished the story his wife had begun.

"It was fun," Maggie insisted.

"I almost missed the football game the next day because I couldn't keep my eyes open." Mac looked to Henry for understanding, and then admitted, "But, yeah, it was fun."

"Next we have the Hilliards."

"The Hilliards are newlyweds?" Mac asked.

"We went to their wedding last February, honey."

Mac rubbed his knuckle along his jawline. "I thought that was a renewal of vows. He's . . . she's . . . well, they're almost *our* age!"

"*That* old? I suppose they should have spent their honeymoon in a retirement home." Maggie rolled her eyes, her dimples framing her sparkling smile.

"If anyone else doesn't know their story, he was widowed. She took care of her ailing mother for years and years," Patsy explained.

"I only bring up their age because I don't know that I'd feel comfortable mentoring someone so close to my own age," Mac clarified.

"Besides, a widow or widower from a happy marriage may need a different kind of support network," Louise said, her thoughts now briefly touching on how she felt after losing Eliot.

The others hummed and nodded their heads in quiet agreement.

"Perhaps that's best looked into after we launch the

program." Patsy set their file aside. "That leaves us with our third applicants. The Wickhams."

"K-Kat and Eggy," Henry said the names slowly, with his eyes moving purposefully from Louise to Mac to Maggie.

"Eggy?" Maggie drew the shape of an egg in the air with her index finger.

"Nicknames, both. Kat for Katrina and Eggy for Edgar," Patsy explained.

"Oh well, now that does make a certain kind of sense, doesn't it?" Maggie reached out and took a cookie, which she promptly offered to Mac.

"Not to me." Mac accepted the cookie. "Edgar is a fine name. *Eggy*, what kind of name is that for a man?"

"Says a man who goes by a nickname himself." Maggie lifted the platter up to extend it toward Louise, then Henry and then Patsy before taking a cookie for herself.

"Thrust upon me at a young age," Mac held up his hands to show he had had very little say in the matter.

"Well, I can see a young p-person not being f-fond of his name." Henry used the back of his hand to swipe away a bit of cookie that fell onto his sleeve. "We all must know p-plenty of people who don't g-go by their legal names, after all."

"Twenty-two," Patsy announced.

"B-beg your pardon, dear?"

"That's how old the Wickhams are—each of them is twenty-two."

"Kat and Eggy, twenty-two." She slid out the folder. "Neither was raised in a church but came to know the Lord as teenagers. They met online and were married in less than a year."

Patsy took a photo from the file that showed the slender Kat sporting obviously dyed red hair that would have done Ethel proud and wearing a satin gown from another era.

"They came to Acorn Hill six months ago in hopes of

working hard and saving up enough money to open their own business one day," Patsy read on. "Because of that move, they have few friends and no family in the area."

Edgar, "Eggy," wore a tuxedo jacket and baggy pants with a red silk tie and black fedora. They looked more like children playing dress up than a pair of people vowing to love and honor each other for their entire lives.

"Kat and Eggy, twenty-two," Louise whispered.

"All in favor of Kat and Eggy?" Patsy's hand shot straight up even as she called for the vote.

Henry nodded to show he had registered her choice, and then he turned his attention to Maggie. She frowned, pushed at the papers on the table before her a moment, then squared her shoulders, smiled and lifted her hand.

Mac seemed to be engrossed in the form in front of him. Or perhaps he had dozed off. A gentle nudge of Maggie's elbow made the man raise his head, look at his wife, and then follow her lead, holding up his hands.

"That's a majority," Pasty announced. "Kat and Eggy will be our first couple."

"This is not a democracy. This is a church committee come together to do what's right for our congregants, dear," Henry reminded his wife. "We should not go forward until we've heard from everyone. Louise?"

She thought of the young couple who had turned to the church to get themselves off on the right foot. "I think we should pick these two," Louise said. "And, though I have to check with my sisters to make sure we don't have anything else going on, I think we should consider Grace Chapel Inn for the test run of the Making Marriage Matter weekend."

"Oh, Louise, that sounds ideal." Patsy looked to her husband, who nodded his agreement.

Louise called the inn. Jane and Alice were delighted to have the group, and the inn was free on one of the weekends the Leys had suggested. Louise took the good news to the committee.

They laid out the details, and then Henry nodded. "Are we all in favor of these arrangements?"

The group agreed to use the inn, which would offer the rooms for free. The church would cover the cost of the food for the weekend.

And Louise now had her own call to duty.

Chapter Seven

On the following Tuesday, Patsy and Henry Ley came to lunch at the inn to discuss the plans for the couples' weekend. They chose a day when Alice, acting as a representative of the church board and the inn, would not be at work. Since Jane had little to do for Mr. Sturgis as they waited for the paperwork on the sale to come through, she volunteered to make lunch, and they asked her to join the meeting so that she could offer suggestions about creating an inviting setting for the event.

"Everything smells so wonderful, Jane. May I help you serve?" asked Patsy.

"If you would, please just make sure everyone has something to drink while I set the cranberry chicken on the table."

"Cranberry chicken?" Alice asked as she sat down. "What? Not Southern fried chicken? Not a chipotle chips and salsa chicken casserole? Not even a slice of Texas toast?"

"Without Lyndon around these last few days, I'm afraid my tastes have reverted to a more northerly flavor," Jane said with a laugh. She placed the serving platter on the table. Fragrant steam rose from the slow-roasted chicken stuffed with cranberries, wild rice and herbs. Next to the platter was a serving dish holding a squash medley in butter sauce.

A basket of fat, moist rolls still steaming from the oven rounded out the menu.

"Eat up folks, but leave some room for dessert. I made a Boston cream pie."

"It all looks so good," Louise said.

"And smells wonderful," Henry said. "I think I may have g-gained three p-pounds just inhaling, Jane."

"If you all like this, I would be happy to make it for the couples during the Making Marriage Matter weekend."

"I know it will be delicious, but, well, I was thinking it might be nice if we prepare some things out of the church cookbook," Patsy said as she arrived with a pitcher of ice water and began filling glasses. "Then we can make a present of the cookbook to the newlyweds. Sort of a welcome-to-our-fold gift."

"I like that." Louise turned to Jane. "And I think there are some recipes of Mother's in that cookbook. Maybe you can do one of those?"

"Sounds perfect."

They said the blessing and had hardly begun the meal when another thought occurred to Jane.

"You know, if the church is going to make a gift of the cookbook, maybe I could provide the gift of a cooking lesson."

"Yes!" Patsy's face lit up.

"I like it," Henry concurred. "In fact, I wonder if it might be a lesson that we could use during the weekend."

"Do you mean that we'd have the young couple prepare a meal, with Jane's coaching, for the older ones?" Louise wondered.

Henry nodded.

"I think that's an excellent idea." Jane looked at Louise, and then in turn each member of the group. "Food is such an important part of how we relate to one another. It's not just how we nourish people, but one way of showing how much we care about them. And you get to know people so well when you share a kitchen and get a meal on the table with them."

"That's an excellent p-point. It makes me think that we should have both c-couples working in tandem." Henry laced his fingers together to illustrate the coming together he envisioned. "It will create a d-different kind of bond from what the course study will provide."

"And it will take some of the pressure off the young folks," Alice added.

"Leave it to you to think of that, Alice." Louise raised her water glass in a salute of appreciation.

"Young people and their issues have been on my mind of late, of course." Alice noticed the Leys' questioning looks and gave them a brief account of Baby New Year.

Henry's face grew somber. "If those new parents want someone to talk to, I would be happy to make a call. Nothing p-pushy, of course."

"Oh, I can't imagine you being pushy, Henry." Alice smiled at him. "But I don't think they would see anyone except maybe the hospital chaplain. They are so very proud and so very alone."

"Those poor dears," Patsy said.

"I wish they had a situation like the one you are planning with the Making Marriage Matter program. Right now they are determined not to ask for help. They feel they have to prove they are mature enough to handle this setback with the minimum amount of outsider input."

"There is something to b-be admired about that, c-certainly. But they have to think about their child as well." Henry stroked his chin, his eyes narrowed in thought. "I tell you what, Alice, if you don't mind, would you at least let them know that if they do need anything, there are p-plenty of good people happy to step up and do whatever is called for?"

"I will, Henry. Thank you." Alice squared her shoulders and raised up her chin. "You just never know what impact a simple decision to serve can make on the lives of others, do you?"

They all answered in agreement.

"Is that something you will be able to discuss in your speech, Alice?" Louise asked.

"Why yes. I believe I can." Alice briefly explained her upcoming speaking commitment to the Leys. "It's not a speech so much as preparing an overview of my experience and some of my philosophies about nursing. Then there will be questions and answers for the panel."

"Do you know who will be on the panel with you?" Jane asked.

"Well, as I understand it, Rachel wants to have representatives from different areas of health care so that at any given workshop there will be between two and four speakers tackling a topic. According to the information I have so far, I will be addressing Issues Faced by Veteran Career Caregivers."

"That's a mouthful." Henry paused from accepting a second helping of squash to go with his second serving of chicken.

"Yes, they used both *veteran* and *career* because they want to make sure people understand they mean those of us who have been in health care a long time," Alice explained.

"You should keep that title in mind when you give your speech," Louise said. "Keep it simple and use your own words. Be direct. Be yourself."

"If I were being myself, I'd just stay in the audience," Alice joked. "Of course, I don't have that option now that I've made a promise to the conference planner and a promise to myself to help that sweet young family."

After she said that, the group went quiet.

"Why don't I take up these dishes, and then bring in pie and coffee? While we enjoy that, I can tell you about my many misadventures running errands for Mr. Lyndon Sturgis."

Jane regaled them the rest of the meal with tales of shopping for Lyndon. "Twice he had asked me to go furniture shopping, once for a sleeper sofa and a second time for a set of matching lamps. I figured I'd find something tasteful, simple and neutral."

"That's exactly what they say to do on all those decorating shows on TV, simple and neutral for basic items and then just a pop of color or a special object to show your personality," Patsy said.

"Exactly. So I searched online. I found the best product for the money, made sure that shipping charges wouldn't be prohibitive, addressed whatever issues I thought Lyndon might have and came up with an assortment of workable solutions."

"And?" Alice leaned in, urging her to tell more.

"And no sooner did I sit down at my laptop to e-mail him my findings than an e-mail appeared in my mailbox."

"He wanted something exactly the opposite of what you found?" Patsy guessed.

"Worse. He'd already rushed out and bought something completely different from what I'd found, in the secondhand shop in Merriville."

They all groaned.

Then, so they wouldn't think of Lyndon as truly bothersome, she ended her saga with a sweet story. "I have to let you know that when I suggested that he commission Sylvia to do a quilt of fabrics from some of his wife's things, so that he would always have a part of her with him, he did not reply by e-mail."

No one said a word but their expression told her they wanted to know what he *had* done.

"He called me to thank me for thinking of the quilt and

then he followed up with a handwritten note." Jane stood and laid her napkin at the side of her plate. "And that's the side of Lyndon that I try to keep in mind when his cost-cutting, impatient side surges to the forefront."

Jane remembered that discussion on Thursday when Lyndon returned to town and asked her to be present at his meeting with the contractor, Clark Barrett.

"Done and done." Lyndon stepped out of the bank patting the breast pocket of his dark blue jacket. "I own the land lock, stock and barrel. Now all I have to do is get rid of the locks, stocks and barrels, if there are any." He clapped his hands together and gave a barking belly laugh. "Mostly I have to get rid of all the dead brush and tree roots."

Jane gave a cautious smile. "I have to say things are certainly clipping along at an astounding pace. Usually when a person buys property, he or she has to schedule closings and meet with lenders and have a big gathering of people signing papers."

"You're thinking of when a fella buys a house and takes out a mortgage. That ain't for me."

"A house?"

"A mortgage. No, ma'am, um, no, thank you. I pay my way as I go, cash money." The tall man cast a long shadow on the ground as they walked together toward his vehicle. "If I can't afford that, I do without until I save up and can afford it."

"Very smart," Jane conceded. "But not always practical for everyone."

"Served me well all these years. I have all I need and most of everything I want. Top it all off, I am in debt to no man."

Jane knew what he meant. He owed money to no one and no one held any financial sway over him. "I thought your daughter and son-in-law would come up with you to see the property before you began clearing."

"Come all the way from Texas? To see a patch of dirt? No. Unnecessary. They've seen dirt." He shook his head and plopped his cowboy hat onto his head. "I've seen dirt as well, but I wouldn't mind riding out and taking another gander at my plot of it, now that it is mine."

"Of course."

"So if this contractor fellow you put me onto would show his face, we could get under way. Where do you think he is?"

Jane turned and looked down the street wondering the same thing. She had asked Clark to meet them at ten. It was a few minutes past that time now. "He should be here any second. He's very responsible, I assure you."

Lyndon thrust out his chin and narrowed his eyes at her. "If you say he's the real deal, then I believe it."

Jane relaxed at bit.

The Texan sucked his teeth, then looked down the street and added, "But if he doesn't show in ten minutes, he's fired."

"He's fired for being ten minutes late?" Jane couldn't believe her ears.

"Time is money, or to put it more accurately, now that we have work on the line, my time is *my* money. I don't cotton to wasting either one."

"I know, but you might be interested in something my Aunt Ethel said recently. She said that people who . . ." Jane took a moment to find a kinder substitute for Ethel's blunt words, "mistake stinginess." ". . . confuse cost-cutting for good stewardship often cost themselves, and the folks they deal with, more time, frustration and money than they save."

"I'm sure your aunt is a lovely woman."

"She is."

"But on this matter, I don't think we would see eye to eye."

Jane decided not to pursue this reasoning with Lyndon.

No, he was the kind of man who had to take his lessons from the school of hard knocks. He probably had a very long learning curve. She would, instead, be there to help him clean up if things did not work out as they should. That's what she had signed on to do by praying not to seek her own way but to do the job that God set before her.

"Four minutes and counting." Lyndon checked some digital device in his beefy hand.

Jane searched the street for any sign of Clark. She swept her gaze from the real estate office to town hall. Then she spotted Clark.

Clark raised his arm and waved to her, something in his hand, and she smiled.

"Lyndon, don't you have to have building permits and whatever the law requires you have on hand regarding professional certifications and permission to have special equipment on your site?"

"Paperwork," he spat out the word the way some men might have uttered a mild curse. "Now I really will let that contractor go. He's not here and your reminder just added who knows how long to my work day."

"Where's the trust you said you had in me and my choice of contractor? Just turn around and see that the reason Clark is a few minutes late is that he's already gotten your paperwork done."

Lyndon did just that.

Clark strode toward them in his usual work outfit consisting of a chambray shirt, jeans and a sport jacket. He had a heavy canvas workman's coat slung over his arm and a dark green folder in his hand. Though not quite as tall as Lyndon, with his dark gray hair and substantial build, Clark seemed a good match for the blustering Texan.

"Well, I'll be. Those papers for me?" Lyndon reached out toward the file.

Clark met his briskness by clasping Lyndon's extended

hand in a firm grip and giving it a shake. "Good to finally meet you in person, sir."

The directness took Lyndon aback. He mumbled a greeting.

Clark let go of his hand, gave Jane a nod of greeting, and then held the file out to Lyndon. "I think you'll find everything in order."

"*Hmm.*" Lyndon accepted the folder and flipped through it.

"Those are for you. I have my own copies. I suggest you keep all your records and receipts in that folder so we can square off when the project is complete."

"Hope you have your own transportation. Once I get out to the site, I plan to stay put." With that, Lyndon tipped his hat to Jane, turned and headed off.

Jane mouthed an apology to Clark.

He shook his head and smiled. "I knew what I was getting into, Jane. Take my word for it, as a contractor I have experienced much worse."

He took a few steps and caught up with Lyndon before the lanky Texan could climb into his SUV. "You know, Mr. Sturgis, I am working this job into my schedule as best as I can. I understand you have a special situation with your daughter expecting and her moving and all."

Lyndon nodded. "Yes. I understand. It's not that I don't appreciate your effort. It's just that we are awfully pressed for time."

"I know that. And I was happy to get this paperwork done for you and to go out to the site and talk over what needs to be done, but I have to be on another job this afternoon and I can't start your project until that one is complete."

"How long will that take?"

"A lot of that depends on the weather, but I'd say a few more days."

"In a few days I could have that lot cleared."

"Well, if you'd like, you can get the land cleared, and I will come in and lay the foundation and put up your A-frame."

"If that's what I have to do to get the ball rolling, yes, absolutely."

"I can work with that. *If* you use a reputable crew and follow my instructions to the letter." He extended his hand again, this time not in greeting but to seal the bargain they had just made.

Lyndon took his hand and shook it. "Okay then. Let's get moving. Daylight's burning."

"Did I hear you say you intend to stay on site the whole time?" Clark asked as Lyndon started for his SUV again.

"Got a TV and DVD player built into my vehicle, a tent rated for subzero temperatures and fixin's for everything but baking a birthday cake. No need to pay good money for a bed I won't hit until the wee hours and climb out of at sunup."

"You're talking about some pretty long hours. Are you prepared to pay the workers for that kind of overtime?"

"If the workers come prepared to do the job and give me a full day, there won't be any cause for overtime. I'll pitch in myself, of course. Wouldn't ask a man to do for me what I wouldn't be willing to do for myself."

Chapter Eight

On Wednesday of the following week, Louise began to feel the stir of expectation for the coming event. While she had not been included in the specifics of the process that Henry planned to employ, he and Patsy had emphasized that they wanted input on both how to make the experience more helpful and on how to model a strong relationship for the young couple.

They had asked if Louise would mind referring to her own marriage as an example, if the need arose. She told them that she would be glad to do so. She felt that if these young people could find the kind of contentment and companionship she had known as a spouse and a parent, they would have the foundation for a long and happy life. Still, like Alice trying to be prepared to cover a multitude of questions that might come her way, Louise wanted to bring more than just her personal experience to the mix.

She went into her father's old study, now the library, to see if there were any books on marriage. As she began to prepare for the Making Marriage Matter weekend, she wanted to bear in mind Ethel's admonition not to assume that only new ideas were worthwhile.

In the library, she found Jane fussing with some oversized,

thin papers that seemed to want to curl into a tube as she tried to look at them. Alice sat with Jane's laptop, scanning a Web site.

"I didn't realize your work would entail reviewing building plans, Jane." Louise peered down at the drawings.

"Lyndon has some leeway in how he can have the place plumbed and wired, and he wanted me to look over these and tell him how I would put the kitchen in order."

"That's smart of him. I hope he doesn't get in so big a hurry that once again he doesn't wait to hear your input."

"There's always hope," Jane conceded, her eyes fixed on her work.

"And what are you doing, Alice? Research for your panel?"

"I haven't even been able to begin thinking about my presentation because I've run into a problem with lodging and I haven't heard back from Rachel Grissom about it."

"Why do you need to speak with Rachel?"

"The person I spoke to did not have the authority to deal with my problem but said she'd make sure Rachel got the message and not to worry about it."

"Not to worry? That's not really very constructive advice."

Alice sighed and squinted at the screen. "That's what I thought, and then I decided maybe it was the best advice of all. I accepted this opportunity to serve the Lord, so perhaps trusting Him about the details is part of that call to duty."

"Well, there is that." Louise couldn't deny the logic in her sister's thinking. Still she asked, "What can I do to help?"

"Nothing, unless you can find me a place to stay for four days."

"I thought you planned to stay with Virginia." Jane finally succeeded in getting the papers flat on the desk and hurriedly anchored the corners with whatever objects she could get her hands on. "What happened?"

"Life happened," Alice said.

"What?" Louise asked.

Alice looked at her older sister. "I made those plans the first week of January."

"Yes."

"When the weather was unseasonably warm, before the roller coaster of weather we've had this month, the light snowy days, the January thaw, and then the sudden drop of temperatures far below freezing."

"Yes, that roller coaster sent poor Lyndon into a tailspin, trying to get his land cleared, being the actual boss of a crew . . ."

"A problem?"

"I can't say for sure. I only know that when I asked Lyndon if he was having any trouble following Clark's instructions, he snapped that he wouldn't waste his cell phone minutes running to Clark for help with something as simple as clearing brush and packing dirt.

"He's really pushing everyone to get things done while the weather isn't too bad. Maybe if you need a place to stay in Philly, you can take a page from him and tent it."

"As booked up as hotels are, I may just resort to that." Alice sat back in the seat, weariness showing on her usually bright face.

"You were telling us that you made your plans to stay with Virginia and then the weather changed? I don't see why that matters," Louise prodded Alice to finish her story.

"Yes, I made my plans before all that happened and, more importantly, before Virginia hooked up her garden hose to the outside faucet to wash her patio on a nice day."

Jane leaned forward over the papers she had undone. "You can't stay with Virginia because of her patio?"

"Because of the hose. She shut it off at the nozzle but didn't turn off the faucet. Then the below-freezing weather moved back in."

"That's not good," Louise observed.

"Not good at all. The water that had collected in the hose backed up into the kitchen, where the outside faucet connects to the internal plumbing."

"So she had a leak?" Jane seemed to be applying this information as she traced the possible path of Lyndon's home plumbing on the house plans.

"She has a mess! The pipes in her kitchen burst while she was out, and water went everywhere. Everything is waterlogged, and a wall has to be taken apart to get it all cleared up, making that whole part of the house uninhabitable."

"I don't see how that affects your staying there," Jane said without lifting her gaze from Lyndon Sturgis' house plans.

"Well, they'll have to turn off the water for an extended period. A period that coincides with—"

"Your planned stay," Louise finished.

"Not good. Not good at all." Jane frowned.

"No," Alice agreed.

"Can't you stay at the hotel where you'll be speaking?" Louise asked.

"I didn't have the conference reserve a room for me, and now the hotel is full." Alice held out her hands. "I can stay elsewhere but I worry about how that will be worked out at this late stage."

"Of course the conference organizers will help you with that."

"It's my understanding that the conference has been plagued by cancellations and mix-ups from the start. They are trying to keep on top of them all, so I think my needing a room is a small issue in the big scheme of things."

"They still want you there, don't they?"

"Yes, but I elected to stay outside the hotel and take my expenses, so my lodging is technically my problem. I must honor my obligation but now I have to consider driving, covering my own parking fees and any added expenses, so it leaves me with less money to give to the baby and his parents."

"It can all be solved in a single phone call, of course." Jane met Louise's gaze.

"I have called but as I said—"

"Not to the conference people, Alice, to Louise's old friend, the one she has been meaning to call anyway."

"Mrs. Pennington!" Louise looked at the books and remembered then that was one of the reasons she'd been thinking of looking into older views on dealing with marital issues. She'd had Mrs. Pennington and her own early marriage on her mind.

"You wanted to call her and for Alice to meet with her to make sure she's all right."

"It would be a nice solution since, unlike any number of your friends in town, I know exactly where she lives and I got to know her when you were neighbors." Alice looked up at Louise inquiringly. "But I wouldn't want to impose."

"Impose? I would imagine that if her health is good, she'd love to have you. If it didn't coincide with the Making Marriage Matter weekend, I'd even go with you." Louise felt a pang of regret that she couldn't do just that. Yes, asking Mrs. Pennington was a good idea.

Within minutes she had her old neighbor on the line.

"Louise Smith! As I live and breathe. How are you?"

"I was calling to ask the same of you, Agnes. When I didn't get a Christmas card from you this year, I wondered if anything was wrong."

"Wrong? On no, dear. I was just so busy. I got greetings out to all my e-pals—that's what I call all the ladies I keep up with through the Internet, you know—no such thing as a *pen* pal anymore."

"The Internet?" Louise was no stranger to Web sites, e-mail and so on. She found them a practical means of everyday information-sharing, but it did take her aback to know a woman she had always thought of as her elder was online.

"Oh yes. I never use snail mail anymore," she said. "In fact, that's how I missed sending you a card. I was on a holiday cruise when I did a whole mass mailing of Christmas letters. I didn't have your e-mail and, well, I just never bring my tattered old address book with me anywhere anymore."

Louise laughed, relieved to know her friend had not changed and still had a zest for life and learning new things. "Now that I know that, I have a favor to ask of you."

"Anything, dear."

"My sister is going to a conference in Philadelphia from Thursday the twenty-fourth through Sunday the twenty-seventh, and the friend that she was going to stay with has had a pipe burst in her home and—"

"Of course they can stay with me, dear."

"They?" Louise was about to tell Agnes that only Alice needed housing but then it occurred to her that Virginia probably would need a place to stay too. It would be nice for Alice to have Virginia as a roomie. "Well, I was actually speaking of Alice, but Virginia might well want to join her. I will pass along your generous invitation. I know Alice will be so grateful for your hospitality."

"Love to have visitors. You know I am so proud of my home and like for people to get as much enjoyment out of it as possible. Now, will you be coming along with your sister?"

"No, I have a commitment here in Acorn Hill."

"Right. Yes. With your inn. How's that going?"

"It's been an enlightening journey. Like you, we're finding joy in sharing our home with others. We love having a full house. In fact, we'd love to have you visit."

"No need to ask twice, dear. I would love to come."

"That's wonderful, Agnes. When would be convenient?"

"Well, I have a built-in house sitter the weekend your sister will be here. Why not then?"

Chapter Nine

"Ladies, if we hope to pull off this ol' switcheroo smoothly, we need to get on the road." Jane leaned against the fender of her car and whipped out a small date book from her purse and flipped to Thursday morning, January twenty-fourth.

"I'm ready. Let's get going. We must reach the halfway point between here and Philadelphia by two o'clock." Alice tapped the face of her wristwatch.

Though they had provided for plenty of travel time, Alice couldn't help already feeling a bit behind. She chalked that up to a restless night thinking of the trip and the conference, and the fact that she had never heard anything more from Rachel Grissom about the check that had not been included with the conference information Rachel had sent. Alice had packed two days ago, trying to imagine every occasion and scenario in which she might find herself over the next four days. She had laid out her travel clothes the night before and gathered together anything else she thought might be of aid to her this morning. Now she just wanted to be on her way.

"Virginia was nice enough to offer to drive Mrs. Pennington halfway over to meet us and to take me back to Philly." Alice finished putting her luggage in the trunk and shut it with a decisive *wham*. "I don't want to keep them waiting."

"We'll be on time," Jane assured her. "But let's make certain we all have the same time penned in for meeting up on Sunday."

"Not a bad idea. We've gone from a slow month with nothing to do to literally having our every minute booked for the next few days." Louise opened the front passenger door and got in. "However, let's do this in the car while it warms up."

Alice gave a shiver that implied agreement and got in the backseat.

Jane slid behind the wheel.

"It certainly was nice of Virginia to do this," Louise said over her shoulder.

"Well, in all fairness, it's a small price to pay for Mrs. Pennington allowing us to stay in her home until the pipes at Virginia's are fixed."

Louise smiled. "I knew she would welcome you if at all possible."

"Possible?" Jane reached out to crank up the car heater and rubbed her hands together near the vent even though it only blew out lukewarm air. "Louise, I think you have vastly underestimated how with it and active your friend remains despite her age."

"Didn't you love her reason for not sending you a Christmas card?" Alice laughed. "You will have your hands full keeping up with her, Louise."

"As if I won't have enough going on with the Making Marriage Matter trial weekend." Louise looked down at the personal calendar in her hand. "I am not too worried about Agnes though. I talked to Henry and Patsy about her, and they are thrilled to have her there to help out and share her insights if she is so inclined. I think she might prove a valuable asset."

"All right, time to get rolling. First, let's make sure we all have the same information." Jane raised up her date book.

"We meet Virginia and Mrs. Pennington this afternoon. Alice goes on to Philly. Mrs. Pennington comes back with us. Anything else today?"

"Well, aside from getting settled into Mrs. Pennington's house, I may go by the hotel. I can check in tonight or tomorrow before noon and visit the vendors and health agency booths there." Alice handed Louise some pale green pages, about the size of a church bulletin, which listed the agenda for the event. "Of course, the two of you don't have to concern yourselves with my plans until Sunday when it's time to meet at the halfway point again."

"We'll leave shortly after noon. The couples should be gone or going by then." Louise handed the agenda back to Alice. "As for today, nothing more on my calendar. My real work starts tomorrow."

"Friday lunch." Jane gave a sharp nod. "I've planned something simple. I wanted you to have the flexibility to be able to pull it together whenever the group is ready for it, rather than trying to prepare something and then making them break for it."

"That's a fine plan, Jane. I think your idea of a fix-your-own-sandwich buffet with some simple sides like pasta salad and coleslaw will be just the thing for the situation," Louise said.

"Yes, and it won't be too heavy so they will be nice and hungry for the meal that I am going to help them make together."

"I really do appreciate everything you're doing for this. The menu planning, the grocery shopping, the cooking lessons." Louise looked over the open book in her hands where all their duties were listed with check marks beside everything that had been done or assigned to be done.

"And don't forget, she's going to keep Aunt Ethel company on Saturday." Alice gave Jane an approving pat on the shoulder.

"I think a day of running errands, maybe a trip to the library and some time visiting Sylvia and discussing decorating ideas for Lyndon's home will do her good."

The Leys had emphasized that the proceedings this weekend needed to stay in the inn unless the participants agreed otherwise. No one thought Ethel would interfere or gossip about the group, but her presence might make people less open or she might later unwittingly share something about what had gone on.

"I intend for us to be out of the house before lunch," Jane told them. "We might even go to see how things have progressed at Lyndon's. They plan to start actual construction on Monday, you know."

"That has all gone so quickly," Alice marveled.

"I don't know. Some days I have felt like it would never end." Jane chuckled as she slid her date book back into her purse.

"I know the feeling. I'm beginning to wonder if this trip will ever begin." Louise gave Alice an amused glance over her shoulder.

"Message received." Jane pulled the car out of the drive and the journey began.

The sisters laughed and chatted along the way.

Less than an hour later they pulled into the parking lot of the Country Table Restaurant, where they had arranged to meet Virginia Herman and Agnes Pennington. The two women had just walked up to the restaurant's front door when Jane parked the car.

Though she hadn't seen her in a while, Virginia looked the same to Alice. The years did not show in her round, cheerful face, nor did gray invade her dark blonde hair. She still wore the comfortable kind of clothes she always had. Today, under a navy boiled-wool jacket, she sported a long, rose jumper over a royal-and-rose patterned turtleneck.

Her chunky beaded bracelet drew the eye as she gestured freely while conversing with her companion.

"Look, there they are. I'd know Agnes anywhere," Louise said.

Agnes Pennington was a woman of average height but one who clearly was anything but your average elderly woman. Her white hair, which she wore brushed stylishly back from her face, had a casual look as if she didn't bother overly much to create the short, coarse waves. Her skin was tanned, probably from the holiday cruise, and she was colorfully dressed. The hues in Agnes' jacket—gold, azure blue, turquoise and rich avocado green—were a spirit-lifting contrast to the drabness of the cloudy day. She appeared much younger than her eighty-plus years.

"I love that jacket she's wearing. Do you think she would mind my asking where she got it?" Jane inquired as she turned off the engine.

Louise waved to her old friend, and then unbuckled her seat belt and gathered her purse, telling Jane, "If she didn't actually buy it in a store on some tropical island, I am sure she will tell you where to get one."

Alice slid out of the car and waved to Virginia.

"You know, suddenly I don't feel as nervous about the prospect of the task ahead of me."

"Really?" Louise asked, pausing to let Alice catch up with them as they walked through the parking lot.

"If a woman of Agnes Pennington's advanced years could sail the high seas and surf the Web, both with seemingly fearless ease, then why can't I get up in front of a few hundred health-care professionals . . ."

Alice's pace slowed.

". . . and give a compelling . . ."

Slower still.

". . . insightful . . ."

Her voice wavered.

". . . noteworthy speech?"

Alice stopped altogether.

"Alice? What's wrong?"

Alice looked at her sisters and put her hand over her thumping heart. "Feeling a little green around the gills again. If I asked her, Louise, do you think Agnes would give my speech for me?"

They had enjoyed their meal and exchanged the luggage without any further lapses in confidence on Alice's part.

"I am so glad to have this time to catch up with you, Alice," Virginia said as they drove toward Philadelphia.

"And I with you. We don't really live that far apart, but it seems life keeps us so busy we never make time to visit each other."

"Remember all the fun we had in school?" Virginia thought for a moment and then added, "Well, not *in* school, that was quite a struggle for me, but when you were here going to school?"

Virginia had also gone to nursing school but had left to attend a nearby college in order to become a teacher.

"I think you made the right choice, Virginia. Being a teacher is something you really have to have a heart for, and clearly you do."

"I see why they chose you for this conference, Alice. You know how to say the right thing."

"I hope you're right about that, Virginia." The closer they got to Philadelphia, however, the more Alice couldn't stop fretting about the conference.

"Yes, it's scary," Virginia acknowledged. "New things often are, but surely you must be looking forward to it too."

"Yes and no."

"Why no?"

"I'm not much of a public speaker."

"You? You have so much to offer, Alice."

"Thank you." Alice ran her fingers through her hair. "I just have no clue what I'm walking into. Not at the conference or . . ."

"Or what, Alice?"

Holding back didn't make sense. She planned to spend the whole weekend with Virginia, so why try to hide the small anxiety she had not even shared with her sisters? "It's silly. Really. I, um, I am embarrassed to admit this but I have some qualms about this entire arrangement."

"I've told you, I don't mind the drive."

"It's not the driving, though I do hope you know how grateful I am you agreed to it."

"I do."

"The problem is that I don't feel quite comfortable staying in a stranger's house."

"You're joking!" Virginia let out a burst of laughter before cutting herself off, her eyes wide. "You're *not* joking."

"No. Why would you think that?"

"Because, Alice, you are part owner of Grace Chapel Inn, someone who doesn't simply welcome strangers into her home regularly, but who seeks them out and invites them in to stay as long as they like."

"When you put it like that . . ."

"Now the shoe is on the other foot." Virginia made the turn into Louise's old neighborhood. "You are the one sleeping under someone else's roof where things are unfamiliar."

"Between the conference and having to acclimate myself to someone else's home, I think I have strayed way outside my comfort zone this weekend."

Alice looked first at the lovely old home that once was Louise's, and then at the even grander one next to it, where

Virginia was pulling into the drive. "If this speaking engage-ment makes me a laughingstock as a nurse, at least I will have inn-keeping to fall back on full time."

"Don't even say that!"

"I was just joking. But thank you, Virginia."

"For what?"

"For reminding me that when you stop being open to new things, you stop growing." Alice looked up at the grand old Victorian home where they would stay for the next few nights. "That's what moved Jane to help Lyndon and it cer-tainly applies to what I'm doing too."

"I am so glad you feel that way."

"Why?"

Virginia shut off the car engine and turned to face her friend. "Because Mark has a surprise planned for you this evening."

"A surprise?" Alice, who had been looking down trying to undo her seatbelt, jerked her head up. "What is it?

"If I told you that then it wouldn't be a surprise."

Virginia got out and led the way up the front steps. Agnes had given her the house key and had shown her around the house when Virginia came by to pick her up. The house, a classic Victorian painted a reddish brown with crisp white trim, had a wide front porch and large doors with lots of leaded glass. Alice gazed up at the home, thinking how little it had changed over the years since Louise was Agnes' neigh-bor. One thing that had changed was the house where Louise and Eliot had lived.

There was a new color scheme, new landscaping, even a new front door. It was lovely, just not as she had remembered it. Alice decided not to dwell on that. Change could be a pos-itive thing, and in this case it meant the new owners were tak-ing care of the house and obviously were enjoying their home.

Alice retrieved her suitcase from the trunk as Virginia had done and marched forward, meeting her friend at the wide front door. Even without Agnes there to greet them, Alice could sense the woman's style and verve welcoming them with fresh colors and modern paintings mixed with antiques from the 1800s and collectibles from thirty to fifty years ago.

The living room walls were a golden yellow. The furniture was comfortably overstuffed with lots of pillows and throws that made the room seem cozy despite the very high ceilings.

"I'm assigned to the room at the top of the stairs on the right. The one to the left of the stairs is ready for you." Virginia started upstairs. "You can look at the rest of the house later. Right now you need to get ready."

"For what?"

"Mark's surprise."

"If you told me what that was then maybe I'd have one fewer thing to feel anxious over."

"Where's the fun of that? When you stop being open to new things, you stop growing." Virginia leaned over and gave Alice's wrist a squeeze. "Now let's take up our things and get them put away. You don't have much time to change before Mark gets here."

Chapter Ten

Mark arrived within the hour, bearing a simple bouquet of flowers for Alice and a box of chocolate-covered cherries for Virginia. It was so like him to have remembered that her friend had a fondness for the confection.

He was such a thoughtful man. Alice kept that in mind when, after they had driven a few minutes, Mark instructed her to close her eyes.

"For how long?" she asked. She felt the car turn, then turn again, then go over a bump and roll to a stop.

"Keep your eyes closed until I come around and open the car door for you, okay?"

Alice heard him open his door. "*Brrr.*" She squeezed her eyes more tightly shut and wrapped her coat more snugly around her as the briskness of the winter evening rushed into the warm car.

Mark's car rocked lightly as he got out of it.

"I feel a little silly doing this," Alice admitted.

"Your uneasiness shall be rewarded, I promise." The door shut.

She had hardly had a chance to settle into the beautiful old Pennington home when she'd had to start freshening up for her evening with Mark. Since Virginia had refused to share any details of the outing Mark had concocted, she had dithered over what to wear. Finally, she broke down and gave Mark a call to ask him to give her some guidelines—dressy, sporty, outdoorsy? She also allowed that she wouldn't mind if he'd drop a hint or two about their upcoming itinerary.

He offered only one suggestion. "Wear something green."

"Green?"

"I like you in green," he had explained jovially. "It sets off the red in your lovely hair."

Alice had flushed a little at the compliment, but Mark's suggestion hadn't really helped her decision-making.

She fussed a bit, and then padded downstairs in her robe and slippers to the kitchen to take her quandary to Virginia. That proved just the ticket as her old friend had reminded Alice that Mark would never put her in a situation to embarrass her or even leave her ill at ease. She encouraged Alice to wear whatever she pleased and leave it to Mark to take her to a suitable place.

"It's a matter of trust," Virginia said.

Alice did trust Mark. She must or she'd give in to the impulse now to pop open her eyes, or maybe just steal a peek, to see where they had ended up.

The passenger door opened, and Mark extended his hand to guide her up and out of her seat.

Butterflies fluttered in the pit of Alice's stomach, which she attributed to excitement, a touch of anxiety and, in truth, hunger. "Mark, you won't lead me through the streets of Philadelphia like this, will you?"

"Not to worry. I got a parking spot just outside the exact place I want to take you."

"So I can take a good look now?"

"Not until you take a good whiff."

"Whiff?"

She heard him inhale exaggeratedly by way of encouraging her to do likewise.

Alice hesitated. She had no idea where they were and who might be watching.

Mark put his hand over her eyes and said, "No peeking until you do." Then he gave a softer series of sniffs, as if to say, "C'mon, be a good sport, give it a try."

Alice inhaled. "I smell . . ."

"Yes?"

"Car exhaust?"

"Maybe we need to get a little closer." He guided her forward. "Now try again."

She didn't have to try. Just her normal breathing brought with it the delicious aroma of fresh bread, tangy tomato sauce and . . . "Pizza?"

"Not just any pizza." He took his hand away. "Look!"

"Martini's!" Alice put her hands to her cheeks. "Oh, Mark. It's where we went on our first date. It hasn't changed a bit."

He laughed at that.

Alice demurred. "Well, maybe a little."

The small red brick building had not changed much but the bars on the large plate glass windows had not been there all those years ago, nor had the "This Is a Nonsmoking Environment" sign. Also, the disclaimer about not being responsible for things stolen from cars in the parking lot and the warning about the effects of alcohol on unborn babies would have been unimaginable years ago. The neighborhood hadn't become dangerous or run down. These were just the kinds of updates that Alice suspected came with modern business in a large city. As much as she loved being here at this moment, she felt a flash of homesickness for Acorn Hill.

Mark pulled open the restaurant door and escorted her inside. Noise, damp heat and the aroma of bubbling cheese enveloped them. The brown faux leather booth benches still looked welcoming. Red and white checkered cloths still adorned the tables, all fresh and crisp as they had been on that long ago night.

Suddenly Alice's homesickness melted away. "It looks as if only days have passed instead of years."

She turned to the man beside her and in her mind his gray hair disappeared. His eyes, while still sparkling with kindness, no longer had lines fanning from the corners. She saw for an instant the young man with a world of possibilities stretched out before him. She felt as she had felt then, that no matter what happened between them, she was glad to be spending time with him.

"Thank you, Mark."

"I did well, then?" Mark waved to signal a waitress that they wanted a table.

The waitress raised the cluttered tray in one hand and pointed to the empty booth in the corner. "Reserved just as you arranged. I'll fly past with some menus in a sec," the curvy, dark-haired woman called out.

"You did very well," Alice acknowledged. "This is a wonderful surprise."

"I thought I gave it away when I told you to wear green." Mark helped her shrug out of her coat.

Alice glanced down at her emerald-colored sweater with gold and rust flecks in the yarn. "I really didn't make any particular connection, especially not with pizza or even Martini's."

"You wore green on our first date," he reminded her with a chuckle as he showed her to the booth the waitress had indicated.

The memories came flooding back as she took her seat. "And you complimented me on it, twice. No, three times."

"Maybe more."

Alice laughed.

"I was a regular master of small talk back then." He sat across from her.

"Small talk? You mean you weren't being sincere?"

"Oh, I was sincere. The reason I recall it so vividly, though, has to do with how much I kicked myself later for blurting it out again and again. Every time we had the slightest lull in the conversation, that just sort of found its way out of my mouth." He lowered his gaze, grinned broadly and shook his head at the foibles of his younger self.

"I think I thanked you each time as if it were the first time I'd ever heard it."

"'You look nice.' 'Green brings out the red in your hair.' Over and over?" He chuckled softly. "Hardly the stuff of sophisticated conversation."

"But perfect for the swanky digs you chose for our first meal together." She held her hands up to indicate the cramped mom-and-pop pizzeria.

"You told me pizza was your favorite food back then."

"Still is."

"Can I get you folks something to drink?" The waitress handed them each a large menu and slid a pad and pencil from the pocket in her bib apron.

"Soda?" he asked Alice.

"Iced tea," she replied.

"You used to like soda."

"Things change," she said.

He gave the waitress their drink order, and they decided on a pizza with the works.

Mark tucked away his reading glasses.

Alice folded her hands on the table.

Mark glanced around.

Alice did likewise.

Mark tapped his foot. He unrolled the flatware in the cloth napkin to his right. He laid out each piece and placed the napkin in his lap.

Alice followed suit.

Finally he looked up, directly at her and said, "You look very nice tonigh—"

Alice bit her lower lip to keep a burst of laughter from sputtering out.

Mark winced. "Some things *never* change, it seems."

"So it would appear."

The waitress brought their drinks and a basket of breadsticks.

Mark picked up the basket and tipped it in Alice's direction. The smell of butter and garlic wafted upward.

"Thank you." Alice helped herself to a breadstick.

Mark set aside the basket and raised his large plastic tumbler. "What shall we toast?"

"How about the things we hope will never change about each other?"

"Our everlasting youthful good looks and charm?" Mark joked.

"Well, of course." Alice lifted her glass to that, and then more somberly added, "Though I had in mind this new and special friendship that has grown between us now that we have found each other again."

"To us," Mark concluded. "No matter what life sends our way, may we always remember our surprising and, uh, *sophisticated* yesterdays, find joy in our todays and assurance that those things will provide the foundation for a friendship that will last far into many, many tomorrows."

"That was lovely! I couldn't have found the words to express my feelings like that." Their plastic cups made a soft thud as they touched rims. "Which troubles me a little."

"How so?"

"If I can't make a toast at a pizzeria with an old friend, how will I ever speak on that panel on Saturday?"

"First, you need to get your facts straight."

"Excuse me?"

"These are breadsticks, not toast." He held one up as if presenting evidence.

Alice laughed at his sweet attempt to put her at ease.

"Beyond that, Alice, you mustn't doubt yourself. You are a thoughtful, intelligent woman who has spent her career caring for others. You've learned so much as a nurse and grown so much as a caregiver and person. You've kept current with medical advances but have not forgotten that human kindness and spiritual connections can make all the difference. What more can I say to convince you of that? What more can I do?"

"You can make the speech for me," Alice whispered.

He laughed. "Alice, this is the kind of message only you can deliver. It's up to you."

"I know." Alice nodded slowly. "It's my call to duty."

"Your . . . ?"

"Here you go. One medium pizza with the works." The waitress slid the steaming pizza onto the table between them.

The mood broken, Alice gave Mark a pat on the hand. "I went into this with prayer and faith. Those will get me through. As you said, I have a good foundation and I should never underestimate how far that will take me."

Chapter Eleven

Before going to the inn Thursday afternoon, Jane and Louise had given Agnes a tour of the town. When Agnes had seen Sylvia Songer's shop, Sylvia's Buttons, she had insisted they stop and the four of them had had a wonderful time talking about everything from fashion to exotic finds that Agnes had collected in her years of traveling. When they did get back to the inn, they had a light meal. Soon after, Agnes retired for the night, so she and Louise had not had much time to chat by themselves.

On Friday morning Agnes had risen early in order not to disrupt her routine. After a light breakfast that Jane had laid out at Agnes' request, the elderly woman returned to her room to perform her daily tai chi, an ancient form of meditative Chinese exercise. By midmorning, she had showered, dressed and descended to the kitchen, where she found Louise going over her lists for the weekend event.

"I'm so pleased to be here, Louise," she said.

"And I'm so glad to have you here." Louise rose to get the cookies Jane had left behind from a batch she had made to take to the construction site today. Louise went about getting the snack ready while nodding at her friend to take a seat. "It has been far too long since we've had a real visit."

"Thank you, dear." Agnes sat at the table as Louise had indicated. "I am so touched that you thought I might have something to offer to your church's program to nurture young marriages."

"I know that's something you are very good at, from personally witnessing your expertise." Louise set down a plate of snickerdoodles, which perfumed the air with their cinnamon fragrance. Louise held up a mug, asking if Agnes wanted some coffee.

"Better not, dear. But I wouldn't say no to sweet milk. Do you remember how to make that?"

"Oh, I hadn't thought of that in years. Cynthia used to love it." Louise set about mixing up Agnes' own concoction, an updated version of what had passed for a treat in World War II, when people had to get by with whatever they had available. Louise mixed together milk and vanilla and a bit of sugar. "It's not as thick or rich as yours was, I'm afraid," she said as she placed the glass before her friend.

"Oh, that's because I used canned milk, just as we did back then, and less sugar, because it was rationed, you know." The elderly woman took a sip and smiled. "This tastes wonderful."

They sat and shared their little pick-me-up snack while Agnes updated Louise on all the things the newest owners of her old house had done. Before they knew it, Henry and Patsy had arrived, introductions were made and the time for leisurely chatting was behind them.

"What's this then?" Agnes Pennington asked as she eyed a file box overflowing with binders and papers that Henry had carried in from the car.

"It's some of the resource material we are evaluating for inclusion in our Making Marriage Matter program, when we go forward with it after this preliminary weekend," Patsy explained.

"*If* we decide to go f-forward with it after this weekend," Henry emphasized.

"Did you say *some* of the material?" Louise asked.

"A few p-pertinent articles, selections from different courses and g-guidelines for various approaches to m-marriage support g-groups," Henry had to pause to readjust his grip on the box.

"We copied from the computer whatever we thought we might use. We also have lots of software and some DVDs, but we know you prefer to keep the inn low-tech to preserve the ambiance, so we left those at home." Patsy pointed the way toward the parlor, then the kitchen, then the library, silently asking where Louise wanted the materials delivered.

Louise pushed open the door to the library and stood back to allow Henry to carry in the box. She looked around for a place that would accommodate the collective wisdom that Patsy thought would serve them over these next few days. She decided to try to clear away the plans Jane had left on the desk.

Henry did not wait for her to accomplish that goal.

Clunk.

He plunked down his load on the floor and then straightened with his hand to the small of his back. He let out a soft grunt. "You might be surprised to know how much is out there on the subject of creating a happy marriage."

"My goodness, how did we oldsters ever manage without all that input?" Mrs. Pennington, who had followed behind the group, stood in the doorway and tipped her head to one side, her eyes gleaming with amusement.

"We had to make do with love, the support of the community at large and our families in particular and to learn from wonderful role models," Louise reminded her good-humoredly. Then she addressed Henry. "That's what I thought we were going to try to do with this program, provide the opportunities for the role models to offer expertise and guidance."

"Maybe we should construct a mission statement," Patsy suggested. She plucked a notebook from the box, took a pen from her purse and jotted down a notation on a blank page. "Once we have one, I can use it for the opening page on the scrapbooks I plan to make for each participating couple."

"Perhaps that's b-best left for later on, dear." Henry rubbed his hands together like a man preparing to dive into his work. "Now let's get these materials sorted out. We can stack them according to how we hope to use them or by subject matter or—"

"Pardon my interrupting that thought, Henry, but I really want to make sure I have a complete grasp of what we're trying to accomplish here." Louise singled out a notebook with the words *Relationship-Building Exercises* handwritten on a label on the front.

She showed it to Agnes, who peered closely at the label and then cast a curious look at Louise.

"I understood our purpose as trying to re-establish old values, harkening back to the times when the community upheld newlyweds and worked with them to start off their home life right," Louise said.

"It is." Henry bent down, retrieved a stack of papers in files and began shuffling through them. "However, we have to establish some kind of p-protocol for the mentors and the, uh, um, *mentees*, um, t-to follow."

"And all this will do that?" Louise sounded skeptical.

"Think of this more as resource material for whatever might come up. The p-principal object for this weekend will be to gather data."

"Data?" Louise peered into the box, not sure what she should be looking for and a bit anxious about her role. "How will we do that?"

"Oh, we found a series of tests . . . we told you about the tests, right?" Patsy asked.

"Yes, I guess I didn't realize those would take place this weekend. They weren't administered prior to this?"

"Oh no. That will take a large portion of Saturday, actually."

"And these?" Louise held up the folder of exercises.

"Oh, there they are!" Patsy took the notebook and opened it. "Icebreakers."

"Ice . . . breakers?" Louise wondered how that applied to making marriage matter.

"Our young couple is so new to our congregation that we hardly know a thing about them, or they about us," Patsy said.

"In my day we had dances and socials and dinner with our families on Sundays." Agnes, standing back from the group, folded her arms over her salmon-pink sweater and narrowed her still crystal-clear blue eyes. "Not to mention shared responsibility and, yes, even hardship. We didn't need to create exercises or take tests to strengthen our relationships. We thought that was what sharing our lives was for."

Louise wanted to give a hearty "hear-hear" to her old friend's wise words, but settled for giving her own carefully worded view of the subject matter. "Is this really the best way to go about getting to know one another?"

"Oh, Louise, young people no longer relate to each other the way we do. You might recall that these two young adults are quite caught up in the Internet. They probably don't have the best of people skills, poor dears."

Agnes sniffed.

Patsy looked her way. "What?"

"Nothing, dear." Agnes faced the looming mahogany bookshelf. "I was just looking at this whole shelf full of knowledge, philosophy, imagination and art, and wondering what would be the best way to know how much of each is contained in them. What would you say, Louise?" She turned with a mischievous twinkle in her eye and asked, "Shall I judge them by their covers?"

"Message received," Patsy smiled and gave a slight bow of her head. "Still, icebreakers will let us get to know them, but given the way young people communicate these days, or fail to communicate, really, they might just find they learn more about each other too."

"I see your thinking, Patsy." Louise avoided saying if she agreed with it or not.

"We're trying to find our way, Louise." Henry put his hands on his hips and frowned at the box. "We have to b-be good stewards of the church's resources. We cannot go to the board and ask for an investment of time and m-money without some kind of hard data to p-present showing how we think we can make a difference."

"Creating a safe haven for the marriages in our congregation is the right thing to do, Henry. The members of Grace Chapel are good people. If we came to them with nothing more than that mission and a plea to join us, they would support that endeavor."

"In their hearts, yes. In theory as well, b-but Louise, you are a p-pastor's daughter. You know it is not just a job of asking p-people to follow in faith. There is a m-matter of accountability for where we lead."

"Yes, that's true." Louise went to the desk and cleared away the house plans that Jane had left there. "How do you want to organize matters?"

"We can use the relationship b-builders if we have a lag or need to stir things up to give the connections between couples a friendly p-push." Henry took the binder from Patsy and set it aside.

"I still think the young people can learn a lot from those," Patsy held her ground.

"I think we might benefit more from a monitored discussion group," Louise said.

"In the long run, the tests are the real focus." Henry emphasized the firmness of his opinion by striking his open palm with the side of his other hand. "We will have our mentor couple also take them to tell us how accurate they are."

"You mean like a control group used when trying to prove a scientific hypothesis?" Louise asked. "The McGuffeys give us the desired results?"

"Yes, then we'll have something to compare the young people's scores to. This will tell us everything we need to know about—"

"Poppycock!"

They all stopped what they were doing and turned to Agnes Pennington.

"Marriage is about people. It's about love and respect and working things through as you go along to strengthen the bond between you. Each marriage is unique, as are the people who embrace it. There hasn't been a test or a program developed yet that can predict what life will throw at folks, and no exercise devised that will give them the only way to respond to that."

"I tend to agree," Louise said.

"Point well taken, Mrs. P-Pennington. This is our first attempt, just feeling our way along. We believe these t-tests will not just g-give insight into this young couple but will p-provide a guide for us when dealing with the couples that p-participate in the future."

"I suppose we can look at these tests as helping to make us better teachers," Louise mused.

"That's all well and good." Agnes raised her birdlike arms in resignation. "I just find myself wondering if along with all this reading and researching and rhetoric, you all might have taken one very humbling truism into account?"

"What's that, Mrs. P-Pennington?"

"That the person who thinks he has all the answers very often ends up learning quite a bit himself from the very students he proposes to teach."

Chapter Twelve

Friday morning, after having enjoyed a pleasant breakfast with Louise while Agnes went about her daily exercise routine, Jane went for a walk and returned to find a message telling her that Clark had been trying to reach Lyndon without success. He needed to talk to the Texan and wondered if Jane might have some idea of how to get in touch with him.

Jane felt a sense of responsibility toward Lyndon as his local go-between and toward Clark for involving him in a job that Lyndon seemed intent on complicating. So rather than trying to phone Clark and then Lyndon, and then trying to get them to make contact, she quickly packaged up the cookies she had made for the construction crew and went out to the property, where Clark's men were scheduled to do some preliminary foundation work.

Clark came over to Jane's car when she pulled into the site. He was carrying a clipboard with a stack of ruffled pages on it.

"I decided to come out and see what I could do in person, Clark," Jane said as she got out of her car. "How is everything going?"

"I hope you didn't think I meant for you to drop everything and run out here, Jane."

Jane tugged on the gloves that had stayed tucked away in her coat pocket most of this warm winter. It had turned brisk overnight, so much so that she wished she had slipped a scarf in her pocket too. "Oh no. I just wanted to see for myself how things are coming along and bring by some cookies for your crew." She looked around and noticed something odd. "Where *is* your crew?"

"I'm afraid they've done all they can for the day." Clark set the clipboard on the hood of his truck. "My, those cookies do look delicious. It was very thoughtful of you to bring them."

"You said you had other projects to get to today, so why don't you take these along? You can drop off the platter by the inn when you get a chance."

"Thank you." He accepted the cookies and moved to put them away inside his truck.

Jane took that moment to survey the site.

Nothing appeared out of the ordinary to her. The brush had been cut down and the debris had been cleared completely away. The ground was bare and packed down to create a flat surface at the top of a built-up spot on the lot. Though she could not see the whole outline of it, Jane assumed that the wooden framework, partially exposed from where they stood, outlined the footprint of the A-frame. This, she supposed, was where they would pour a concrete slab to create the foundation for the structure.

When Clark returned to her side, she said, "Your crew has made some progress, though."

"*Hmm.*" Clark's mouth thinned to a stern line. He picked up the clipboard again, took a few steps, and then turned and paced the length back to the truck again. "I'm afraid it won't be enough for Mr. Sturgis. I don't expect him to receive the news gladly that it's unwise to press on and pour the concrete today. To top things off, I can't reach him on his cell."

"I'm not surprised." Jane snuggled more deeply into her coat. "He keeps the thing turned off so not just anyone can call him and eat up his time and his minutes."

"I see. Yes. That sounds like him." Clark nodded and cocked his head thoughtfully. "I left a message. Does he usually respond to those in a timely manner?"

"You should know by now, Clark, that Lyndon does everything in a *timely* manner, but it's always in *his* time."

The contractor frowned at that. "The problem is I am working him in between other jobs, and I can't babysit him through everything. I know he hired a reliable crew to prepare the ground. But the ground doesn't feel right to me and I am not going to pour something as vital as a foundation until I have spoken to him and made sure he followed my instructions to the letter."

"That's a sound decision, Clark."

"That's why I've been trying to get in touch with Lyndon. Have you had any communication with him lately?"

"I've gotten e-mails. I haven't checked yet today but the last I heard from him was Wednesday."

He frowned. He cleared his throat. He lowered his gaze. He rapped his knuckles on the back of the clipboard.

Finally, he mustered up a congenial laugh at himself and raised his hands in mock surrender. "No sense hanging around here then."

"So, if I should hear from Lyndon or get in touch with him, what do you want me to tell him?"

"Well, I'd really like to have his reassurance that he followed my instructions and to learn if he has any explanation for why the ground doesn't feel right, but I need to be the one who addresses those issues with him."

"Feel? You said that before. What do you mean?"

"I don't know how to describe it, but an area near where the foundation will be laid just doesn't seem right. It's close enough to the foundation that it could cause problems sooner or later. Sooner, if we pour concrete and the warm weather doesn't hold as it's curing." He held out his hand to invite her to walk around the foundation and see for herself. He strode purposefully at her side, and then extended his hand to steady her as they used boards laid out like tracks for workers to walk upon to make their way up the slight incline.

"Would it be all right for me to walk around the perimeter of the framework?" Jane made a circling motion with her index finger. "I'll stay on the board pathways."

"That's fine. The ground shouldn't be muddy, but better to stay on the boards to prevent ruining your . . ." Clark's gaze dropped. He looked puzzled. ". . . um, boots?"

"Like 'em? Très fashionable, huh?" Jane stuck out her foot to show off her rugged and roughed-up brown suede hiking boots. "I picked them up at a flea market last fall when Sylvia Songer and I were hunting for fabulous finds."

"I don't know that I'd call those fabulous," he joked.

"I thought they'd be perfect for wearing on wet spring days in the garden."

"And for stomping around building sites?"

"Exactly!" She gamely leapt from the board where they stood to the board that led to the right of the foundation. She tried mentally to conjure up the floor plans she had been studying.

She wished she had some paper to make notations on. She dipped her hands into her coat pockets. She found a pen and a roll of breath mint candies.

"Need something?" Clark called.

"I, um . . ." She spotted something pale and pink stuck

to a twig and flapping in the breeze. "No thanks, this will do."

She hopped off the board and strode about five feet away from the framework. Her knees wobbled on the uneven surface. The seemingly packed-down dirt felt oddly spongy under her feet.

Snap.

Crack.

"Should I hear very soft crunching as I walk?"

"Now you know what I mean by it not feeling right. Could be small roots that have been dug up by the heavy equipment hauling brush away, or gravel. Or it could be a problem with how the ground was prepared. It's a dishonest builder's trick to use the brush and debris on site in place of spending the money and time to use more loads of dirt."

Jane stooped down and scooped up the pink page. It bore the logo of a fill-dirt and gravel company, though the information on it had all but been destroyed by the elements.

"*I suggest you keep all your records and receipts in that folder so we can square off when the project is complete.*" Jane recalled what Clark had told Lyndon the first day they met.

She wondered if she should save it for Lyndon; then she noticed it had a line through the final tally and had clearly been wadded up. "I bet he wheedled them into giving him some outrageous discount."

"What are you doing?"

"I just want to make a few notes and I'll be right back over there." Jane drew the outline of the foundation and then oriented it by sketching in landmark trees.

If she couldn't convince Lyndon to make adjustments based on how people most conveniently use a kitchen, maybe he would consider it for some other reason that the drawing would reveal to her. Modifying the pipe placement so he would save money on connecting to the water source? Placing the doors and windows so that he could rely on crosswinds and sunshine to cut cooling and heating costs in summer and winter? Something would come to her, she knew it.

"The kitchen should be about here?" She stabbed her pen toward the eastern corner at the back of the foundation.

"I believe so. Do you need a set of the plans?"

"No, no. I have them back at the inn. I'm just trying to get oriented." Satisfied, she stuffed the paper in her coat pocket and picked her way back around, board by board. "This will do for now. I want to talk to Lyndon about the way things should be laid out."

"You deserve some kind of award for tackling this job with Sturgis." Clark rubbed his hand over his forehead.

"He's not that bad, really, especially when you realize he lost his wife of many years not so long ago and now his daughter is moving away. I suspect that's behind the gruffness and impatience."

"Ah, I didn't know that. It does help to put up with his eccentricities knowing a bit of his story, doesn't it?"

"I think that can be said of most people." Jane scanned the building site with admiration for what Lyndon had managed under the stressful circumstances of working sometimes long distance, sometimes having to rely on, and blindly trust, total strangers.

"Thanks, Jane. You seem to have a knack with him."

"Well, I believe you can learn something from every person you meet. I'm learning all sorts of things about Texas, for example, and about what kinds of treasures there are to be found at the secondhand shop in Merriville," she said brightly. "Just to name a couple of things."

"Yes, I can attest to that. I've learned a few things about going green from him as well." Clark chuckled. "In fact, I think he's used more repurposed material on this job than on any other one I've ever done."

"Repurposed?"

"Scraps, salvage, refinished, recycled."

"Ah." Jane nodded. "And I thought he'd stretched the limits when I proposed a color scheme for the place and he informed me he'd paint the place entirely with 'oops paint.'"

"Oops paint? You mean he's going to decorate with the paint store's mistakes and customer castoffs? For his home?"

"His *vacation* home," she reminded Clark, as if the fact that the place wouldn't be a full-time domicile made it a tiny bit better.

"Still." His forehead furrowed.

"Yes." Jane didn't have to hear him spell out that he knew someone with her artistic sensibilities would find the decision to use random and rejected colors befuddling. "It's been an eye-opener for me."

"Really? I'd think oops paint would make it something you'd want to address with your eyes closed," he joked.

"I'm afraid that's how it will look in the end, as if someone decorated entirely in the dark." Jane feigned covering her eyes, giggled at the thought of it all, and then let her hands fall to her sides.

Clark gave an amiable shrug.

They shook hands and agreed that whoever spoke to Lyndon first would urge him to contact the other.

As Jane got back into her car, she marveled at where Rev. Thompson's sermon had brought her. She tried to recall a quote from C. S. Lewis that she thought Louise had once shared about prayer not changing things but instead changing us.

Louise would know the exact quote, or exactly where to find it. Jane wrote the words "prayer changes us" and "C. S. Lewis" on the paper. Then she reread her shorthand version. "Prayer changes us," she murmured.

She liked that idea. As she drove away from the site, she thought that the same could be said of serving others. It changes us and the world around us.

That thought brightened her day.

Chapter Thirteen

While Jane was with Clark, Alice and Virginia were at the conference site, browsing among the vendors' booths.

"Thank you for letting me poke around the displays with you this morning, Alice."

"I had two badges, Virginia, and I knew you'd find all this fascinating."

"I feel like a kid at the country fair," Virginia said as she nodded to thank a lady who handed her a yellow collapsible cup with the name of a popular prescription medication stamped on the lid.

"I feel like the world of medicine is now moving so fast it might just be passing me by, leaving me behind."

"You? No, Alice. Never. You love your work and are always learning new things. You'll never be left in the dust because you won't stand for it. You want to keep up and even get ahead of the crowd for your patients' sakes."

They looked around at the vast array of booths, displays, tables, demonstration areas and even individuals strolling along handing out pamphlets and advertising giveaways.

Alice scanned the room. So much to see. So much to hear. So much to carry!

"Welcome to the vendors showcase, ladies. Please take one of our reusable totes to hold all the information—and goodies—that interest you today." A very pleasant young woman dressed in a colorful scrub top and pants handed Alice and Virginia tote bags made of different styles of cloth from a medical uniforms company she was promoting.

"I wish I could just fill this bag with every new bit of information and keep it with me all the time." Alice raised her tote. "Then I'd be ready for anything."

"You *are* ready for anything, Alice, with what you have in here," Virginia tapped the side of her own head. "And in here." She lowered her finger to her heart. "If you don't know something, you find it out. If what's called for is beyond a purely medical solution, you get creative and get things done. That's why they invited you to speak here."

Buoyed by her friend's faith in her abilities, Alice still had to protest. "I'm here because they had a slew of last-minute cancellations and I happened along when the event coordinator came through the hospital."

"A hospital filled with candidates to recruit as speakers." Virginia gave Alice's shoulders a wobble as if she could literally shake some sense into her. "But the coordinator chose you to come here and share your expertise with these good people."

Alice took a deep breath and nodded in acceptance. "Then I suppose I'd better let these good people know that I've arrived."

At the far end of the huge convention space sat a stage with two long tables with eight chairs facing outward and a podium. Immediately to the right of the stage was a row of chest-high columns. Each had a partition around it to create some privacy. What these were piqued Alice's curiosity, but her real interest was directed to the left.

Two long tables arranged in an "L" shape were staffed by several professionally dressed people checking papers, handing out packets and giving directions. The bold red-letter banner above all the activity read: Registration.

"You go take care of that, and I'll start filling up my goody bag." Virginia held it open. "This makes me feel like a kid going trick or treating."

"This place looks more like a medical Mardi Gras to me." Alice looked around, her pulse kicking up with excitement over the mix of hubbub and promise around her.

"Look for me in the first aisle when you get done, then." Virginia started off.

"Will do." Alice gave a wave and then went to report in for the job she had committed to do.

Five minutes later she was at her friend's side.

"That was fast. Where's your speaker's packet? When do you speak?"

"Your guess is as good as mine."

"I don't understand."

"You got it right when you compared this place to trick or treating. Only I'm the one who seems to have gotten tricked. For now, at least."

"Is something not right?"

"Not so much 'not right' as not formalized." Alice looked longingly toward a side room with a sign posted outside that proclaimed: Speaker's Lounge. "My panel has been canceled!"

"Oh dear! Does this mean you'll be heading home?"

"No. Actually, they want me to stay. They hope to plug me in someplace else, but they aren't sure where yet. And since they don't have a place for me, there isn't much for me to do."

"Can't you go to workshops?"

"The panels this afternoon are all about insurance and lectures about the latest medicines and that kind of thing. Very little of that applies to me." Alice held out her hands to show how helpless she felt. "To further complicate things, since they don't have me scheduled to speak, they don't have a check for me. That's why I didn't get my per diem ahead of time. All my financial arrangements are on hold."

"Oh no. What will happen?"

"They assure me they will pay me my expenses at the very least, but no one here seems to have the authority to do that. They left a message with the coordinator, but she's in a meeting."

"Do we have to leave the floor and return our goodies?" Virginia did not actually stick out her lower lip and pout but she did have a note of disappointment in her voice.

"No way. You can hang onto your finds, Virginia." Alice reassured her friend. "This part of the event is open to anyone with a badge." Alice put her hand over the laminated card hanging around her own neck. "So we are in and can stay as long as we like."

"Do you mind?"

"Are you kidding? You're the one who pointed out how much I love learning new things, and I'm the one who thinks she has a lot to learn. This is like a dream for me." Alice swept out her arms to indicate the crazy confetti of health-care services, providers, pharmaceutical companies and more. "Besides, they *will* get this sorted out, and I must stay sharp for when they come to me and give me my assignment."

"I hope that happens."

"I am counting on it. And so is that sweet young family who will benefit from the money I will be paid when I carry this through."

They spent the next hour wandering from booth to booth, listening to vendor after vendor.

Virginia collected pens and measuring tapes and water bottles stamped with logos of the companies handing them out.

Alice gathered handouts and brochures. She asked people tending the booths to write down information and contact names on their business cards for her to reference later.

Virginia loved coming up with creative ways she could use the promotional items in her kindergarten classroom. She and Alice chatted about how much she had learned to make do, now that she had gone from working full time in a public school to teaching half days for a private church school. They reminisced about how when they were younger, they hadn't always had all the luxuries that people took for granted today, but they had always had so much love and fun.

Despite the mix-up, Alice found her time on the floor surprisingly well invested. In fact, she could have spent the rest of the morning doing more of the same, but when she and Virginia rounded the end of an aisle that emptied out parallel with the registration counter, someone waved to get Alice's attention.

Alice excused herself from Virginia, saying, "It looks as if they've gotten things straightened out. I knew they would. I came here because I surrendered my service to the Lord. I knew He wouldn't let it come to nothing."

Alice hurried across the room only to return moments later after speaking with the person who had signaled her.

"Back so soon?"

Alice took her friend by the elbow, turned her to face the strange columns to their right and began walking in that direction. "Rachel, that's the coordinator's name, won't be available for a while. She had to go to the airport to pick up two of the main speakers for tomorrow."

"You'd think there would be someone she could send to do that."

"Poor thing, she's had all sorts of cancellations for this event and has ended up doing things herself to make sure they don't go any further awry."

"Speaking of going awry . . ." Virginia tugged her arm out of Alice's grasp. "Where are you taking me?"

"One nice person working registration had an idea, and it may take some time, so I don't want to lose track of you."

"Just as well, I guess. My goody bag runneth over. What's the idea?"

"They can't give me a check just on my say-so, but they could cut a check for the end of the conference if I can get the hospital to send them something confirming that I work there."

"Oh, that has to complicate things."

"Apparently they expected me to have arrived with something more than my bright smile and readiness to serve."

"Like what?"

"I was supposed to have been sent a form with an official registration number on it, but I didn't receive it in my packet."

"Can I do anything to help?"

"Will you stay with me in line so I don't have to look for you in all that crowd after I send this?"

"Sure."

"Thanks. I know the hospital won't send anything immediately, given proper channels and that kind of thing. So, after this I'd really like to break away from here and check back later to see if it's resolved."

"Fine. I don't think my tote bag can tote much more anyway." As evidence Virginia spread the handles of the bag wide and a neon-pink chip clip tumbled out.

Alice bent to retrieve it, and as she stuffed it back among the goodies, said, "Oh, the fun isn't over yet for you. According to the people at check-in, these computers are free for anyone. For the good deed of bringing me down here and waiting through all this with me, why not reward yourself with a little free Wi-Fi Web surfing?"

"Free what?" Virginia stepped up as they moved close to the head of the line. "I've heard of hi-fi and YMCA but never Y-fi."

"W-I, not the letter *Y.* Stands for wireless fidelity. It's what they call wireless Internet connections. They said we can check our e-mail, send digital photos or upload video of our visit here in Philly."

"How fun!"

A station came open.

"You go first, Alice. You have official business."

"Come on and share the station with me," Alice coaxed her friend. "I don't want to have to figure this out by myself."

In a few minutes they had not only sent Alice's plea to the hospital but had also sent greetings to Louise and Jane. Next they checked to see if the parts the workers had ordered for Virginia's kitchen plumbing had arrived. Alice sent a note to Mark at the zoo to tell him the story of how she had suddenly found herself with some free time. She asked if he wanted to get together for the afternoon.

"And they have software programs that can track a patient's entire medical history," Alice found herself telling Mark.

She and Virginia had met with Mark for lunch at an elegant café that stood where Alice and Mark had often met for fast food when they were young. When Mark produced a camera, Alice and Virginia raised their water glasses in salute for the photo. Then Virginia played photographer and got a terrific shot of Mark and Alice together at the table.

After lunch, Virginia headed over to her house to see if the workers, whom she now knew had the right parts in hand, were getting anything done.

"Where to now?" Alice asked as she settled herself in Mark's front passenger seat.

"Wrong question."

"*Hmm?*"

"You shouldn't ask where to now, but *when* to."

"When? You mean we're going to go sightseeing?" Alice paused to try to think of the best way of reminding him that she had seen the historic places in Philadelphia many times over. "You know, as much a fan as I am of American history—"

"American history will have to wait." He carefully pulled the car into traffic. "What I have in mind is more of a personal nature."

"Personal?" Alice shifted in her seat, unsure what to make of that.

"Personal *history*," Mark explained as he headed off down a tree-lined side street. "Forget the Liberty Bell, the Betsy Ross House and Independence Hall. This afternoon we are not going to visit the places that shaped the nation but the ones that helped make us the people we are today."

The rest of the day went by quickly as they reminisced about things they had done and the effect their time together here had on their future lives. Alice got misty-eyed seeing the hospital where she had done most of her clinicals while in nurse's training.

They drove by the home of the veterinarian who had taken Mark under his wing and encouraged him to keep working toward his dream. Though that man had died a few years before, he was alive in Mark's memory. Alice was fascinated by some of the stories Mark told about this wonderful man.

Finally they went to the park where Alice first told Mark that she couldn't envision a future with a man who was not Christian. That decision on her part had, in time, set them on entirely different paths in life.

"I was such a blind fool." Mark walked past the bench where Alice had taken a seat. He gazed off at the sidewalk that disappeared into a cluster of winter bare trees. "Not just to let you go but not to have been open to the message of salvation."

"You came to the Lord in time. That's what matters now."

"Have I ever told you that I considered just going through the motions back then? Joining your church, telling you that I had changed my beliefs?"

"I am so glad you didn't try that. I'd have known. If not right away, then with time. Our relationship would have been predicated on a lie and, in time, that lie would have created a rift between us."

"You are right, of course."

"Have I ever told *you* that some small part of me wished you would have done just that, just to have gone along with my expectations."

"Really?"

"Yes, but that was only a small part of me. I talked to Father about it. Cried on his shoulder. He told me that it was better this way, and that in time I would come to respect you more for having been truthful, no matter what the cost."

"And was your father correct?"

"You know he was." A lump formed in Alice's throat as she thought of that time. Her emotional reaction didn't last long, and she turned her attention to Mark again and reminded herself that the life they each had now was good.

"I have tremendous respect for you, Mark. That's why, after all this time, I feel that we have the makings of a wonderful friendship."

"It doesn't hurt the cause that I became a Christian." He snapped a picture of her on the bench. "But then, you always thought I would, didn't you?"

"Are you asking me if I had faith in you that you would, well, have faith? Or are you asking if I always hoped and prayed that you would find your way to the Lord?"

"Either." He looked at her, at last without the camera raised, a twinkle in his eye. "Both."

She thought about it. It only took a fraction of a moment for her to conclude, "I knew you were a good man. I knew you were seeking the way. And even long after we had parted, I never stopped praying for you."

He grinned.

A young couple appeared, walking hand in hand as they wandered along the sidewalk.

Mark's expression grew more pensive. "I can't help thinking that if we had kept in touch, given things a little longer to work out . . ."

Alice held her hand up. "We agreed when we reconnected as friends that we wouldn't try to imagine what might have been."

"But sitting in this park—"

"No. Please don't go there," Alice said softly. "That was what it was. We can build on it, starting with a solid friendship."

"That's best. Don't forget the past. Use it as a foundation." He held out his hand to help her up.

"Don't let it keep you from making the most of the present." She took his hand and stood, slipping her arm in his as they walked back to the car. "If you can do those things, there is no reason to feel wary of the future. You will have what it takes to face whatever comes your way."

"I like the way you think, Alice Howard," he said. "I can see why they picked you to come share your wisdom at the conference."

"I don't know about that. In fact, we ought to go back to the hotel to see if they have a speaking assignment for me, or I won't be sharing anything but a car ride back to Acorn Hill and not a cent for little Baby New Year and his struggling parents."

Chapter Fourteen

I t had grown decidedly brisk by Friday evening, but the weathermen, who had modified their forecasts every hour on the hour, had finally announced that the cold wave would blow through overnight. More moderate temperatures would return before the end of the weekend, they said.

It was, perhaps, those assurances that had led the group on the inn's front porch to wear light coats and to carry with them the kind of compact luggage that would not accommodate bulky sweaters or a pair of snow boots.

"Hello and welcome," Louise said as she held the door open for them. "I hope you will all find your time with us pleasant and the Making Marriage Matter sessions productive."

"Thank you, Louise," Henry Ley said as he unwound an overlong and heavily fringed scarf. Louise recognized the muffler as Patsy's handiwork, something unsold from a Christmas craft bazaar held last November.

Her gaze moved quickly on past the Leys.

She raised her hand in greeting to the McGuffeys. The mentors were at the back of the group, he head and shoulders above his wife and she bearing something delicious-smelling in a rectangular plastic container.

Louise homed in on young Mr. and Mrs. Wickham. After looking at their wedding photos and discussing the information on their application, she had begun planning for their arrival in particular. For the last twenty-four hours she had silently rehearsed using the nicknames Kat and Eggy so that when she said them she would not sound or feel silly. She also had prayed for them.

She did not know exactly what to expect, only that they would not be the type of guests that usually crossed the threshold of Grace Chapel Inn.

And they most certainly were not—if appearance and apparel were to be taken into account.

Edgar—"Eggy"—met her gaze. He grinned to reveal teeth so dramatically white that it put Louise in mind of a movie star. He whisked off his blue wool beret and gave a bow graciously in her direction. "Thank you for having us, Mrs. Smith."

When he straightened up again, he tucked a wayward strand of his longish dark hair behind his ear and then folded his hat to fit it into the pocket of his black-and-white checked sports coat.

Louise was impressed that he, unlike many young men these days, realized that it was poor manners to wear a hat inside. She had a sudden feeling that she might like this Eggy fellow, might like him very much indeed.

When he took his hand from his pocket, his coat shifted to one side to show a white button-down shirt and paisley suspenders. He had on gray baggy dress pants and high-top sneakers that gave the slightest squeak on the porch as he shuffled sideways to let his pretty young wife step over to peer into the open door.

Kat raised her hand to give a skittish wave. "Hi."

The scarlet red hair she had sported in her wedding photos had faded to the color of tomato soup but with the odd streak here and there of a dusty pinkish hue.

Louise acknowledged her with a smile and a nod of her head.

"We're excited to have this chance to get involved in a church program so soon after joining," the young woman held her hands together, displaying the fuzzy knit fingerless gloves she wore. She had an oversized coat thrown across her shoulders. "This project seems so perfect. We love people. We love Acorn Hill. We love the Lord."

"We kinda like each other too," Eggy kidded as he slid his arm around his wife's slender waist.

"Eggy!" Kat rolled her eyes but clearly took delight in her husband's attention. She nabbed her coat by the lapel to keep it from sliding off. Louise could see she wore a dress in a style that Louise herself might have chosen in her own youth: tasteful, periwinkle blue with a small floral pattern and a lace-trimmed Peter Pan collar. Though Louise would never have paired the dress with the hand-painted red, green, yellow and turquoise cowboy boots and bright pink, patterned tights that Kat sported.

"But we do love each other, that's for sure," Kat went on to affirm her husband's claim. "And we'd like to do whatever it takes to stay together. We know we have a lot to learn. We don't know much of anything about being part of a church family or trying to make a Christian home. Still, we're so ready to begin."

"Good." Knowing how much you did not actually know was, to Louise's way of thinking, one of the most promising traits a student could possess.

"Then let's get this underway." Henry gave a thunderous clap.

"Oh yes, let's!" Maggie McGuffey chimed in cheerfully.

"Don't stand out in the cold, come in, come in," Louise said with an expansive gesture toward the hallway.

"Here come the brides . . ." Patsy entered singing.

"Well, I'm hardly a bride after thirty-four years of marriage, Patsy." Maggie came to a halt, whatever baked goods she had brought held high and the porch light bouncing off the soft curls of her blonde hair.

Patsy turned to speak, preventing anyone else from coming in. "Oh, I'm sure Mac still thinks of you as his beautiful bride."

"Only because it's an old habit that he is loath to break." Maggie laughed, her bright eyes sparkling with fun over her husband's reluctance to embrace new things.

"Is that a jab about my not wanting to come here until after seven?" Mac sounded more exasperated than cross.

"It wasn't a jab. It was a joke," Maggie said softly but insistently.

"I always watch the Channel Nine *Action News* at six o'clock, followed by the network broadcast." Mac launched into what sounded like a most reasonable explanation in support of his point of view. "I've already missed the lead story and the first weather check."

"L-last report I heard said the cold front will b-blow through overnight," Henry offered as if that might just put an end to the man's mild irritation over the disruption of his typical evening routine.

"If we could just get settled into our room so I could catch what's left, I'd appreciate it, that's all," Mac said. "Then I'd be more than happy to get on with the rest of the weekend. Until the eleven o'clock news, of course."

Louise pursed her lips. She needed to inform the elder example-setter that they had no TVs in the rooms. However, she hesitated to do so right now for fear of what kind of example he might set upon learning that his routine was about to be upset even further.

The group fell silent for a moment.

Louise shifted her weight from one foot to the other, trying to think of how to disperse the building tension.

"I've got an idea, Mr. M." Young Edgar Wickham stepped

up and took charge. "Let's me and you do this up right and carry our brides over the threshold."

"Do . . . what?" Mac cocked his head as if to show he hadn't quite heard that suggestion. Or maybe that he hadn't quite believed it.

"You know. Like on your wedding night. New beginning, old custom." To everyone's surprise, except, perhaps Kat's, young Eggy reached down and swooped his new wife's feet right out from under her. He held her high against his chest and grinned.

Kat giggled and blushed.

Maggie gasped in delight.

Henry Ley chuckled softly at the deftness of the younger man's diversion. Even so his hand went to the small of his own often ailing back, perhaps in readiness to explain to Patsy that he wouldn't be following suit in the wife-carrying department.

Though not the kind of display of impetuous affection with which she'd have been at ease, Louise couldn't help herself. She gave the smallest of sighs at the romance of it all.

"It's time to commit to a new beginning in your marriage, so carry your bride over the threshold." Patsy giggled and stepped aside to make way, motioning Eggy forward with both hands. "Of course, no one expects that kind of grand, romantic gesture from our older marrieds."

"Oh my!" Maggie practically yelped in surprise as her husband lifted her up in his still-strong arms.

"The McGuffeys are still very much in love, thank you very much," Mac informed them all. "And not afraid to show it either."

The couples came inside laughing and the husbands settled their brides on the floor again.

"All right then, let me show you to your rooms." Louise wondered when she should mention the no-TV situation and decided to show the Wickhams to their room first and then to speak to Mac quietly afterward. "If you'll bring your luggage and follow me."

Eggy reached out and snagged the gym bag he and Kat had brought, with the name Wickham written on it in laundry marker, and a black leather attaché case with brass clasps on the bulging outer pockets. He threw his shabby bag over one of his shoulders and cradled the leather bag across his chest.

"Sorry. We don't have a bellhop." Louise smiled. She knew they weren't expecting the kind of service they'd get at a fancy hotel nor did it bother them to carry their own things.

"I'd haul your piano up the stairs on my shoulders, Louise," Mac announced. "If I could just get up there and catch the scores before the news goes off and some game show starts up."

Louise stopped at the foot of the stairs. She couldn't, in good conscience, keep the truth from Mac any longer. "I'm sorry about this, but beyond a very small set we keep tucked away in the kitchen, we do not have televisions."

Mac looked at Maggie.

Maggie did not look the least bit inclined to listen to him complain about this.

"Hey, that's cool," Eggy piped up just then. "Sounds like fun, even. Charges up the old think-juice to break away from the TV monster now and then, right?"

Despite the newness of their marriage, Kat had already learned how to give Eggy what Alice liked to call "the eye" when describing the way a wife looks at a husband when she isn't exactly happy with what he has just done or said.

"What?" Eggy seemed to know instinctively how to respond in the way most husbands did. He took on an air of innocence and inability to understand what was wrong. "I can go a weekend without watching the tube."

"The tube, maybe." Kat gave a purposeful shake and her coat slipped off her shoulders. She caught it in one hand, swung it around and draped it over her arm, never taking her gaze from her husband. "But what about *YouTube*? What about playing video games? Can you go a weekend without those?"

"Oh, I have my laptop." Eggy hugged the leather case closer.

Suddenly Mac leaned in and asked, "You can't pick up TV on that thing, can you?"

Eggy smiled. "I can view downloaded shows after they've run."

"That will work." Mac put one hand on Eggy's back and used the other to gesture toward the table in the entry way. "Let's take a look at what you've got there."

"Fellows, p-please. That's not wh-wh-what . . . wh-why w-w-e . . ." Henry got more agitated by the syllable.

"We came here to get away from these kinds of distractions." Maggie folded her arms and let out a long, low breath that matched the deflated expression forming on her previously carefree face.

"Tell me about it," Kat muttered, reaching down to pick up the gym bag her husband had dropped on the foyer floor.

"Hi, everyone. Dinner will be ready in ten minutes," Jane appeared from the kitchen with an aura of relaxed congeniality. Her timing proved excellent.

"Dinner! Great!" Mac slapped his hands together and then rubbed them to show his satisfaction. "That way we can watch the TV in the kitchen while we eat."

"Watch TV while you eat? I think not." Though never a mother or a school teacher, Jane had the authoritative tone down pat.

"Just like home." Mac ignored her and slipped his arm around his newfound television-watching buddy's shoulder.

With an open-handed gesture he directed Eggy to make a beeline for the doorway behind Jane.

"Our guests do not eat in the kitchen, Mac." Louise tried not to appear snappish and exasperated. The weekend was hardly getting off to an auspicious start. "We will serve you in the—"

"Poppycock!" Agnes Pennington came down the stairs spouting her seemingly favorite word.

Louise recalled that when she was younger she'd found Agnes' word funny, endearing even. Tonight it did not carry for her much of that old-fashioned charm.

"There is nothing that breeds familiarity more than sharing a meal in close quarters. Eating in the kitchen family style on a blustery winter evening? What a wonderful way for folks to get to know one another." Agnes reached the bottom step.

Louise glanced at Henry.

"W-well I sup-p-pose we could—"

"You can all crowd into the kitchen, if you please." Jane folded her arms and did not budge. "But dinner will be served in the dining room as planned."

For a moment, Jane's declaration left them all silent.

"You know, Agnes, there is also much to be said for gathering in the dining room, where someone has gone to great pains to see to your comfort and pleasure, where one has nothing to worry about but enjoying the meal and lively conversation." Louise extended her arm to show the way to the dining room. "We'll save eating in the kitchen for another time."

"Dinner will be served in ten minutes." Jane backed through the door, as if by turning around she might inadvertently invite the others to follow her.

"Ten minutes? Does that give me time to put these things away and wash my hands?" Kat asked.

"Me too." Maggie stepped forward and presented her

container. "If you don't mind. This is for tomorrow evening's dessert. It should be refrigerated"

Louise accepted it. "I'll show you to your rooms and then you can wash up. You should have just enough time before we eat."

"And that will give us time to check out this laptop of yours," Mac said to Eggy.

Louise looked around for a place to set Maggie's gift; then she finally handed it to Patsy and asked her to put it in the refrigerator.

Agnes stepped aside to allow the women to go up and in doing so caught a glimpse of the laptop as Eggy withdrew it from his case. "Oh goody! I wanted to bring mine but I didn't think the inn would be wired for it. If you don't mind, I'd love to check my mail and maybe dash off a note on my blog about the goings-on around here."

All eyes turned to the white-haired, eighty-something woman.

"What? Why so surprised?" She smiled coyly. "A girl has to keep up with the times, doesn't she?"

"You have a blog?" Eggy laughed, not cynically but in a show of undisguised delight. "Cool. My name is Eggy, uh, Edgar Wickham, by the way."

"Agnes Pennington. Call me Agnes. And it's good to meet you, *b-t-w*," she casually used the Internet shorthand for the phrase *by the way* that Eggy had just uttered.

"And you have a blog, you say?" Eggy went back to setting up his laptop while Mac and Agnes looked on and Louise directed the women up the stairs.

"ATGBwithAgnes," she rattled off. "Stands for 'As Time Goes By,' the song that was playing the first time I saw my husband. Of course, he wasn't my husband then, although by the time that song was over . . ."

Agnes' voice trailed off, roughened by emotion. The

power of that emotion, and Louise's curiosity about Agnes and her husband's love story, made Louise pause on the steps.

But Agnes did not continue her comment, choosing instead to *ooh* and *ahh* over what Louise could tell was a state-of-the-art laptop. "Oh yes, this is top drawer. How many gigs? Is that the latest DDR3?"

Mac stood back and shot Maggie a look that showed he was duly impressed with Agnes. And the laptop. He gave a thumbs up that implied he was much happier about the whole weekend commitment now.

Maggie sighed softly.

Eggy chuckled and said to the older woman at his side, "You really know your stuff."

"I think that if you aren't afraid to try new things, you will always keep learning. And nobody is too old to learn something new."

Louise smiled slowly and shook her head. "I guess if one is never too old to learn, this weekend will hold lessons for us all."

They shared the wonderful meal that Jane had prepared. She had kept it simple, not knowing the tastes of the couples. The first course was a refreshing salad of butter lettuce with sliced oranges and strawberries and raspberry vinaigrette. The main course was a delicate pasta in a light cream sauce flavored with basil and grilled vegetables on the side. Jane had baked small loaves of bread that each couple could break together, an old Italian tradition that says that bread must be broken, never cut, and that sharing it strengthens relationships.

After dinner, Henry gave them an overview of the Making Marriage Matter concept. He thanked them for agreeing to help the committee learn how to best serve their congregation. Afterward, he used Eggy's laptop to show a short film about marriage and the church, and then he and Patsy headed home.

Louise excused herself to do her Bible reading before turning in. When she left the group, they were huddled around the laptop, getting lessons from Agnes on how to attract "hits" to one's blog. This weekend, Louise concluded, was going to be memorable for one and all.

Chapter Fifteen

I am not here to give a concluding speech," Alice said with a sigh. She had reported to the conference on Saturday morning confident that the organizers at last had gotten everything in order. "I was asked here to participate in a panel."

"Yeah." The young man at the registration table did not lift his head from shuffling a stack of papers in his hands. "That's what I said. You're slated as one of the four speakers giving the concluding remarks."

All the vendors had folded up their booths, and half a dozen housekeeping personnel were busy clearing away the trash and vacuuming.

"How can I *conclude* anything? I have no idea what I would speak about."

"Says here your topic is 'Keeping Perspective by Keeping in Touch with Your Personal Commitment to Healing.'"

"Keeping perspective?" she whispered. That was something she wished she could do right now.

"By Keeping in Touch with Your Personal Commitment to Healing," the fellow repeated the second part of the title of her supposed talk. "The, uh, the sentence underneath says, 'A seasoned professional shares from personal experience how to avoid burnout and keep patient care and personal job satisfaction at an optimum.'"

"A seasoned professional?"

"That means you've been around awhile," he said.

She jerked her head up, startled at his completely non-chalant bluntness.

He didn't even bat an eye at her response.

Perspective, she reminded herself. A young man in a rush probably had no idea that emphasizing a woman's age might offend. He wasn't telling her something she didn't already know, after all.

Still, it did make her long for a more tactful time as well as help her to appreciate a gentleman like Mark all the more. She must have stood there mulling that over for more than a few seconds because finally the papers went still.

He raised his head. "Oh, that's not a bad thing, you know, the whole seasoned-professional tag."

"It's not?"

"Naw. Conferences like this depend on the sharing of insights from people who have blazed the trails, you know, uh, undergone trial by fire."

"Trial by fire is one thing," Alice said with a rueful smile. "This is quite another. More like trial by jumping out of the frying pan *into* the fire."

"Huh?" He scrunched his fresh face into a look of puzzlement.

Whrrrrr. Whumph. Thump bump. Whrrrr. A housekeeper came bustling around them with her industrial vacuum on high.

Alice shook off her anxiety. "I was just joking. Do you have any idea how I can get in touch with Rachel?"

"She'll be in here around three."

"Three?" Alice looked at the clock on the wall. "It's 9:15 now. Are you sure I can't get a hold of her until three?"

"We can probably get her a message but I can't guarantee she can get back with you right away. I do know for sure she'll be here around three."

"For sure?"

"Yeah. She's the one moderating and emceeing the concluding presentation. In fact, they want you to be here then anyway so you can make sure Rachel has your credentials correct for your introduction."

"My introduction? For the concluding presentation?" Even speaking the words aloud herself could not make them real to Alice.

"Yep. Four o'clock. This room." He pointed with his pen. "On that stage."

"That stage."

"At four." The paper rustled. The man did not make eye contact before he pivoted and simply walked away to the far end of the table.

Alice folded her hands together and watched as two young men in hotel uniforms rolled in two carts piled high with metal folding chairs. The contraptions rattled to a lumbering halt, one on each side of the room where booths had once sat.

Three more men appeared, and all of them began setting up the chairs. Row after row. Enough chairs to fill more than half of the room and all of them facing the stage from which Alice was expected to speak.

I don't think I can do this. She could hardly swallow just thinking of it. How would she ever work up enough gumption to get up those stairs and speak to a room full of medical colleagues?

What am I supposed to do now? Faith and good intentions had put her in this predicament. God would not forsake her until her mission had been accomplished.

Should she spend the day trying to come up with some

words worthy of a seasoned professional? Or should she attend sessions to hear what others were talking about? Or should she seek out Rachel and tell her she could not possibly get up and speak?

"Okay then, just this one last detail, Ms. Howard." The young man returned.

Alice realized that he hadn't just walked away from her but still had been in the process of helping her.

"Now that we've gotten everything in order, I am authorized to give you this." He held out a thick envelope. "Rachel made sure they got your name printed on the check too, so you're all set."

Alice took the large envelope the young man offered her and absently muttered, "Yes. Thank you."

"Oh and, uh, the note with it from Rachel said to make sure to tell you if—since you don't have a room here in the hotel, that is—if you wanted a quiet place to get away to work on your talk, you can use the speakers' lounge."

"The . . ." Alice swiveled her head slightly and saw the room she had noticed on her first day here. "Oh. Yes. Thank you."

Then it dawned on her that maybe someone in there could help her. Maybe someone would have advice for her. Alice turned in the direction of the lounge, but stopped when the young man added, "No one will be in there since most of our speakers are leaving early or will be in sessions all day."

Alice's shoulders slumped.

"Okay, Ms. Howard? If you don't need me for anything else, best of luck. Got to run, duty calls."

"Duty calls," Alice repeated softly. She had entered into this for all the right reasons. Why had it all gone so awfully awry?

She glanced at the rapidly growing rows of metal chairs turned to face the stage. If things didn't get straightened out, she would be standing up on that stage in a few hours and those chairs would be filled with conference attendees.

Quickly she marched to a bank of phones, and in short order she had called Virginia and Mark and next found herself on the line with Louise.

"I am so glad to hear your voice, Alice. I really wish you were here today."

"Oh?" Alice set aside her own concerns for a moment. "Why?"

"Well, Jane has gone off with Aunt Ethel. They are going to do the grocery shopping, drop their purchases off here and then stop by Sylvia's Buttons to pick up Sylvia. Then the three of them plan to have themselves a girls' spa day at Sylvia's home, complete with beauty treatments, herbal teas and chocolate truffles before Jane returns to host the couple's cooking session."

"Girls' spa day? Tea and chocolate? I could do with some of that myself."

"Maybe we'll have her plan something for us after the Valentine's rush is over next month," Louise suggested.

"Absolutely!" Alice could practically feel the tingle of a refreshing facial on her cheeks while she propped up her feet for a pedicure and snuggled into a warm bathrobe.

"It's nice that she will be relaxed and refreshed before she dives into the meal prep. We've asked her to instruct but to let the couples do all the work."

"Let someone else do all the work? In her own kitchen?" Alice clucked her tongue. "I can see why you wish I were there, to keep Jane from helping by jumping in and doing it all for them."

"There is *that*, but I also could use a hand with these husbands."

"*Hmm.* Never having had a husband, I am not sure what help I'd be."

"You may never have had a husband, but you've certainly done your share of keeping men in line in your work at the hospital and also with Father when you took over running the household in the last years of his life."

"Father really wasn't difficult to care for, Louise."

"No, but like most men, he was inclined to want to have things his way and sometimes needed a woman's hand to, let's say, 'nudge' him along."

"Nudge? Are you saying the men are not being cooperative?"

"Only by default."

"Default?"

"Yes, if they don't get to do what they want, *de fault* is all mine," Louise said.

Alice chuckled. "Very clever."

"I can't take credit for it. Agnes came up with it."

"How is she doing?"

"She's fine. Spry as the youngsters, and every bit as hard to keep in line as the men."

Alice laughed again.

"I tell you, Alice, it's all I can do to keep them from watching TV or connecting to the Internet or staying up until all hours playing computer games on Edgar Wickham's laptop."

"What are Kat and Eggy like?" Alice asked.

"For the most part, just darling and fun, very polite."

"Oh, that's encouraging."

"They dress as though they got ready by digging through a pile of cast-off clothing in the dark, but on them, the things look rather sweet and old-fashioned."

"That helps me visualize them a bit, at least," Alice said with a laugh. "Your little weekend endeavor probably won't do much for their fashion sense, though."

"No. I'm not sure how much we will do for their relationship either."

"*That* doesn't sound encouraging."

"I just . . . did you know that they met online?"

"Really?"

"I see this young man who is practically glued to his laptop and this young woman who is, well, so young. I wonder how well they really could have known each other and how well they will *get* to know each other under these circumstances."

"It seems to be the modern way of doing things."

"So does discarding marriages at the drop of a hat when they don't turn out to be everything one imagined," Louise reminded her.

"Sad but true."

"If you ask me, a marriage should be based on getting to know someone over time, learning their likes and dislikes and then moving forward, slowly."

"Courtship," Alice said in a quiet voice, thinking about Martini's and the café and the park, those places where Mark had courted her years ago. "But even a lengthy courtship cannot ensure that a relationship will work out in the long run."

"Indeed," Louise said, snapping out of her pensive mood. "Oh, but I haven't even asked you about the conference. Have you taken part in your panel yet?"

"Not until four today."

"Four? I'll hold a good thought for you then. I really do appreciate your taking time from your schedule to call in for an update on things around here."

"Oh, this call is ever so much more than wanting an update, Louise." Given that opening, she let her words all rush out at once. "I'm in real trouble here." Alice filled in Louise about what had gone on at the conference.

"Oh my! You should have spoken up right away. Have you called Mark? Is Virginia with you? What can I do?"

"What can you do? You can do what you do so well. You can pray with me, Louise."

"Yes. Of course."

"Pray the Lord's prayer with me, Louise."

"The Lord's Prayer?"

"I just need to speak the prayer Jesus instructed us to pray. I need to hear the words. I need to find my foundation and then I feel sure I will know what to do next."

"Yes. Yes, that's a good idea. Let's pray."

"Okay." Alice bent her head and closed her eyes.

"Our Father, who art in heaven, hallowed be Thy name," Louise began.

Alice joined in, and from that point they spoke as one, their hearts and hopes resting in every word.

"Thy kingdom come, Thy will be done, on earth as it is in heaven. Give us this day our daily bread. And forgive us our debts, as we forgive our debtors. And lead us not into temptation, but deliver us from evil. For Thine is the kingdom, the power and the glory for ever and ever. Amen."

Silence followed as they both absorbed anew the truth and beauty of the words.

Alice cleared her throat to keep her voice from breaking with emotion, and then she murmured, "Thank you for being there for me, Louise."

"Well, I wish I could actually be there *with* you."

"You just wish you could run away from all those people trying to have their own way in your house," Alice teased.

"You could be right," Louise admitted. "I thought when I took this on that I would have more input, more to contribute besides fetching refreshments, keeping the men from sneaking into the kitchen to watch TV, and trying to smooth things over after Agnes' assessments of what is and isn't 'poppycock.'" Louise's soft laughter proved that she was, in fact, rather enjoying the challenge. Even if that challenge was not exactly what she'd signed on for.

"I wish I shared your outlook on situations like this, Louise. I know I encounter all sorts of things as a nurse, but for that I have my training to fall back on. I know what must be done. I know the goal is to provide the very best of care for each patient according to his or her needs, to give my all, to help and heal. But this isn't anything like that."

"Isn't it?"

"What do you mean?"

"Alice, you came into this with patient care in mind. If you think about it, the topic you were prepared to discuss . . ."

"Issues Faced by Veteran Career Caregivers," Alice filled in when Louise let her voice trail off.

"Yes. If you think about it, that topic isn't all that different from being the voice of the seasoned caregiver discussing how to keep a fresh perspective."

"That's true." She might not have written anything yet for the new topic, but she did have the basics already in her notes.

"You volunteered to try something new in order to help a child and his family. Now you have been given a wonderful opportunity not only to do that but also to entreat others to go out and do the same. It's like bringing a little bit of God's kingdom to this world."

"On earth as it is in heaven," Alice repeated.

"Think about it, Alice. I know you can do this. God knows you can do this. Otherwise, you wouldn't be where you are right now."

Alice thanked her sister and hung up the phone. She sat for a few seconds trying to believe what Louise had told her.

What do I really have to offer all those people? Why would the Lord choose me to do something so clearly out of my realm of experience?

She walked into the speakers' lounge and sat down. Glancing down at the envelope on her lap, she slid open its flap.

One tug brought the materials out into the open, and on top of them was a check made out to Alice Howard for considerably more money than she had expected. Attached to the check was a note.

Dear Alice,

I am so sorry for the confusion that has kept you from being able to participate in the conference in the way we had agreed. I know this is an imposition, and if you absolutely cannot do the new presentation, then I understand. I am sorry that I have missed your messages and that we could not connect via phone, but I want you to know how much I appreciate your stepping in like this. When the hospital e-mailed us with your information, the secretary mentioned you wanted to donate your fee to the fund for the New Year's baby who had so many health issues.

Even though I have only met you once, I was not in the least surprised at your motivation for giving up your weekend to pitch in and help. I saw in you (and in the way the nurses who work with you daily described you) the kind of caregiver that we should all aspire to be: humble, enthusiastic and with an open and willing servant's heart.

God bless you, Alice, for your work and your inspiration. Please find enclosed my own contribution and one from my company. I am proud to add what I can to the collection for little Baby New Year.

Sincerely,
Rachel

PS: It occurred to me that you might not check back in at the computer banks again now that this is sorted out, so I am including this note that came via the e-mail with your confirmation. It is information from the hospital, updating the baby's condition.

Alice flipped up the letter to read the latest bit of what turned out to be some of the best news she had had all month.

Just then Mark and Virginia walked through the door. Their faces lit up when they spotted Alice.

Virginia waved enthusiastically. "We're here. What can we do?"

Theirs was one of the finest examples of simply reporting for duty that Alice had ever seen.

That, along with the note, the prayer and the reality that she had gone into this to be able to give to a family so very much in need made her pause.

Rachel was right, God had already blessed Alice. She had a wonderful home and so many people who loved her and would help her without hesitation. She had her education and experience. She had warm memories. She had a foundation to build on.

Her mind's eye filled with the image of Baby New Year and his family surrounded by love and leaving the hospital together at last. Along with that picture, she could hear Louise's voice uttering the Lord's Prayer.

"I think, I *hope* I can do this."

"That's the way, Alice." Mark put his hand on her shoulder.

"Remember, just because things aren't going the way *we* want to doesn't mean they aren't going exactly according to . . ." Virginia lifted her eyes heavenward for a moment before finishing ". . . the plan."

"Thy will be done," Alice murmured. She had signed up for just that, to follow God's will to the best of her ability. She took a deep breath.

Alice had answered the call to duty for all the right reasons. Surely she could rise to the challenge. She would take a step forward in faith. "Let's find a quiet spot and put our heads together. We have lots of work to do if we are going to pull this off."

Chapter ✦ Sixteen

"All right, everybody, move closer together for a photograph." Patsy bent her knees to get the whole group in the shot. They sat at the dining room table after Saturday's breakfast and before they got involved in the plans and objectives for the day. Louise had just returned to the room from taking Alice's phone call, and Jane had finished clearing away the remains of her hearty offering of blueberry pancakes, breakfast quiche, sausage, bacon, granola, fresh fruit and yogurt. "Something for everyone," she had told Louise as she prepared the menu. Now she was tidying up the kitchen as the group got down to work.

Henry stood at the head of the table with a large dry-erase board propped up on an easel at his side and piles of file folders in front of him. He frowned as he asked, "Are you sure you want to do that now, Patsy?"

"We must preserve the memory. Years from now, maybe at Kat and Eggy's twenty-fifth anniversary party, someone will be grateful that we took time to record this little gathering."

Henry folded his arms, making the soft knit of his gray sweater bunch up across his chest. Unlike the rest of the group, he and Patsy had the chance to go home last night and returned this morning wearing clothing more appropriate to the change of weather. "Cold and blustery," the weatherman had described the day.

"If you don't want to think that far ahead, then what about the church at large?" Patsy gestured with her powered-up digital camera for emphasis as she spoke. "What about the board?"

"What about them?" Mac asked. He stretched slightly before he covered his mouth with his fist to hide a yawn. He lowered his hand, however, in time to show just the hint of a smile cross his lips as he joked, "You're not planning on calling them in here for a photo shoot too, are you? Because I bet you'll have to drag some of them, the ones who work hard all week, out of their nice warm beds."

Eggy laughed at that.

Maggie reminded her husband, "I know you usually sleep in on Saturdays but this is for a good cause."

"I'm just saying," Mac went on, still walking the fine line between grumpy and jovial. "If you were to try to take pictures of the other members of the church at this hour on a Saturday morning, you'd preserve a lot of memories of people in pajamas who haven't even combed their hair yet."

"See, I told you I wasn't the only one who sleeps a little later on Saturdays." Eggy turned to Kat.

"You're supposed to be setting an example," Maggie whispered to Mac, though everyone in the room could hear.

"And the example I'd like to set is one of a man who works hard all week and catches up one day of the weekend."

"Nine o'clock is not a 'little' later," Kat muttered to Eggy. "I get up at a quarter 'til six every morning, seven days a week, in order to exercise to stay healthy and fit."

"P-please, everyone, could we settle down?" Henry asked. "We really need to get started if we're to accomplish everything we have planned for today."

Without another word, the group got up and moved in close, forming a perfect pose for the photo.

The flash went off.

"Thank you." Patsy gazed down at the view screen in her small camera, beaming. "That's a wonderful shot."

The group moved back to where they were before the photo.

"Good. On to business. As you can see, I've divided the day into m-manageable segments." Henry gestured to the board. "We have several blocks of time set aside for lessons on things like c-communication styles and applying biblical p-principles in marriage."

"We also have some fun learning and bonding activities," Patsy chimed in with a wave of her camera.

"Yes, and then there are the tests." Henry tapped his pen on the spaces set aside for those. "Not to worry though. Poor grades on those won't become a part of your permanent record."

The group laughed politely, perhaps a bit nervously.

Nobody liked being tested. Louise understood that.

While she approved of trying to put everyone at ease, she wondered if the suggestion that they might do poorly hadn't actually put the group more on edge.

"We have gleaned the b-best selection of tests from several programs," Henry forged on. "Th-that we, uh, um, found on, uh, from . . ."

He tugged at the collar of his sweater. His gaze dipped. He moved to the stack of papers on the table and lifted up one file and then another as an example. "Uh, l-like th-this one and, um, here's a-an-an a d-different one."

Patsy's gaze never left his face. Her lips twitched as though she wanted to speak up and fill in the blanks for him, or at least fill the awkward silences. She did neither. She just waited and watched. She did not step on her husband's authority as a pastor or on his male ego by interrupting.

Hers was a wonderful example of how to show love and

respect for a spouse. The little scene before her convinced Louise that this project could do so much good.

Then, as if he had just remembered what he wanted to say, Henry jerked up his head and spoke more clearly. "We hope they will help you learn how well you know each other and help those of us offering support know how to b-best foster better communication." Henry nodded to Louise to take up the next point.

"And to provide the committee organizing this with some hard data as well as opinions and personal assessments to bring to the church board," Louise said. "I have to take a moment here to tell you, Henry, how very impressed I am with your plan and how grateful we all are for the amount of work you have put into this."

Mac started the applause that followed.

"Thank you b-but that round of applause goes right b-back to every one of you for your willingness to pitch in with this fledgling endeavor." Henry gave them all a nod of acknowledgment. "Now that b-breakfast is over, we will have a short prayer to dedicate our efforts and this undertaking to the Lord."

Louise reached for her Bible, as Henry had asked her earlier if she would read from 1 Corinthians, often called the "Love Chapter."

"Now we'll send our two couples into four different rooms to take the first of a series of tests, each on his or her own."

"*Two* couples?" Mac braced his forearms on the edge of the table and leaned in to better study the information on the board. "You mean you want Maggie and me to take the tests along with Eggy and Kat?"

"Yes, I mean exactly that, Mac."

"But we're the old guys."

Maggie sat up and took notice of that. "Speak for yourself!"

"Old *hands*," Mac corrected himself. "The experienced ones."

"That's exactly why we need you to take all the tests along with our newlyweds," Patsy said.

"We must get a firsthand evaluation about how thorough these tests are." Henry lifted one multipage booklet. "We'd like your take on how well the tests do what they're promised to do."

Mac did not look entirely convinced.

"You and Maggie are in a perfect position to give an opinion if one test seems more in line with our church's values than another," Louise added.

"And you can probably tell us a few things about the tests and process that the rest of us haven't even thought of yet," Patsy chimed in. "Henry and I have taken all sorts of these things to help him better understand his role of counseling others."

"All right," Mac nodded. "I can get behind those reasons."

Maggie patted her husband's hand.

"These tests will supply c-critical fact-gathering information. Each one should give us some insight into the n-nature of your marriages based on b-backgrounds, c-common goals, spiritual needs, financial expectations and more." Henry shuffled through the stacks of paper, occasionally holding up the front cover of a sample test. "Once you have c-completed today's battery and I've uploaded the information into my computer, which I can do while you're, uh, um, fixing dinner, I will come away with some evaluations and a couple of n-nifty graphs that will give us a grasp of who you are as a couple, how your relationship is working and any c-concerns looming on the, uh, on the horizon."

Henry stopped and looked toward the dining room door.

Louise swiveled in her seat to follow his line of vision and, seeing nothing, asked. "Is something wrong, Henry?"

"No. N-nothing is wrong, I was just waiting for Mrs. Pennington to stick her head in the door and shout 'poppycock' at my conclusion."

Louise laughed, and then explained, "Oh, you won't hear that word for a while. Agnes is busy doing her tai chi, I believe."

"Isn't she a hoot?" Maggie asked as the others laughed at Henry's spot-on imitation of Agnes' familiar outcry.

"I like her," Eggy agreed. "She actually showed me some things about HTML formatting that I'd never seen before."

"She is full of surprises," Patsy said. "Was she always like that, Louise?"

"Yes. Always young at heart. I hate to admit it but when I lived next door to her I thought of her as *Old* Mrs. Pennington, and she was certainly younger then than I am now."

"Isn't it funny how our perspective on those kinds of things changes, just as the face looking back in the mirror does?" Maggie stood to reach for the crystal pitcher sitting at the center of the table. She raised it up to see if anyone else wanted water and all declined. As she poured herself a glass, she went on, "Did she and her husband act as marriage mentors for you back then, Louise?"

"Well, their example did, and Agnes was always available to listen and help, but I hardly knew her husband, in fact."

"Really?" Kat, who had tied back her hair in a ponytail with a multicolored silk scarf, asked, "I thought that not knowing your neighbors was a new thing. Sometimes I feel guilty thinking people my age are the first ones that don't know everybody on the block or in their apartment building."

"I knew Agnes very well, Kat. I knew most of the women on my street. That's the way things were. When we had get-togethers, the women usually ended up in the kitchen and the men in the den. Or in summer, the men around the bar-becue and the women . . . still in the kitchen."

Kat looked shocked. "If I'd been you, I'd have come storming out of that kitchen and have given those men a piece of my mind for excluding us."

"*Excluding* us?" Louise laughed. "As often as not we had ducked into the kitchen to get away from our husbands."

"Away?" Kat crinkled up her nose in confusion.

"This isn't part of the official program, but let me give you the benefit of my experience, Kat." Louise leaned in, wanting to let them all know what she was about to say did not reflect poorly on her dear Eliot, but was a tidbit about husbands and wives in general she thought the young woman needed to hear. "There are so many roles a husband plays in your life, but he is not, and *never* should you try to make him, just like one of your girlfriends."

"Hear, hear!" Maggie cheered and Patsy echoed it.

"Back then we had men's groups and women's groups and clubs and activities that allowed the genders to let down their guard and relax or learn or whatever they had in mind without having to worry about how they might appear to the opposite sex."

"There is something to be said about making those kinds of connections," Maggie said.

"You still make those kinds of connections. You just moved the location to card tables in the living room and called it Bunco night," Mac said.

"You fellows have your ball games and afternoons fiddling with things in the garage," Maggie reminded her husband sweetly.

"In answer to the question that started all this, Maggie," Louise said, "I didn't know Woodrow Pennington well. We just greeted each other, but once, for his wedding anniversary, he asked me to play 'As Time Goes By' so he could sing it to Agnes."

"He sang to her on their anniversary?" Kat asked in a

youthful, breathless tone that let everyone know how enchanting she found the gesture.

"Hey, I sing to you," Eggy protested.

"Commercial jingles to remind me of things you want from the grocery store do not count," Kat said shaking her head good-humoredly. "He sang *their* song to his wife. You've never sung *our* song for me."

"We don't have a song," Eggy told the group.

"Lots of couples don't have special songs," Mac said.

"I gladly agreed to play the song," Louise continued. "But other than knowing Mr. Pennington was a bit of a romantic and a baritone who struggled to get through a song better suited to a tenor, I really knew very little about him or their marriage."

"We should ask her," Kat said to Eggy. "I bet she has some stories to tell."

Louise pursed her lips. She should have asked Agnes more about her husband over the years. But when Woodrow Pennington was still alive, it never came up. Later Eliot had died, and other people's marriages were not a common topic of conversation. Then Louise had moved to Acorn Hill.

When Agnes was widowed, Louise would never have presumed to bring up the subject out of respect and for fear it might open fresh wounds.

"Along those lines, everyone, men and women, being able to have time away from each other . . ." Patsy looked to her husband as if to ask if she should proceed.

He held up one finger to ask her to hold off. "All right then. Back to the focus of our day."

The group quieted down and scooted their chairs in, attentive and ready to begin.

Henry turned to look at the board again. "This evening we have the meal the couples are preparing together. Is there anything you want to tell us about that, Louise?"

"Jane has left to do the grocery shopping, based on the menu the group has chosen from the church cookbook," Louise told them. "She'll drop off the supplies on her way to her other activities today. She'll be back later this afternoon to help organize the meal preparation."

"Speaking of meals," Henry said. "We have something special planned for lunch. Patsy?"

Patsy smiled at the group. "I had a bit of inspiration from Louise's inviting her former neighbor here."

"Mrs. Pennington inspired you?" Louise asked.

"Not Mrs. Pennington herself so much—that's not to say she isn't a sheer delight—but even before you mentioned the way people used to get together in your old neighborhood, seeing her, and most importantly, *hearing* her, and seeing how precious it is that you two have maintained those old ties made me think of how much collective wisdom we have in our midst. I think we should make use of it."

This intrigued Louise. She would never have said anything, but she sometimes wondered where people like her or her sisters could fit into the Making Marriage Matter equation. "What do you have in mind, Patsy?"

"A ladies' lunch and a boys' night out, as it were, only at lunch."

The group exchanged glances.

"In s-short, the women will have their lunch together from eleven thirty to noon and we m-men will share lunch from noon until twelve thirty. We hope that will give us time to talk, to b-bond, that sort of thing."

"I love it!" Maggie exclaimed.

"I'm with you, Maggie. I think lunch with just us women sounds fabulous," Kat spoke up.

"I think it's all *fabulous*. I am so happy to get to take part in this weekend." Maggie's eyes lit, her dimples framing an eager smile. "Don't you all find it exciting?"

"Yeah. It's a regular thrill ride," Mac droned, his eyes twinkling in fun.

Maggie stretched up out of her chair, leaned over and gave her husband of so many years a kiss on the cheek. "Have I told you how proud I am of you coming along this weekend?"

Mac muttered something inaudible to the group and pulled away, but only slightly.

"Thank you, Mac, for putting up with all the disruptions to your routine for the good of this program and to provide a safety net for Kat and Eggy."

Mac grinned at his wife and in his eyes you could see that even after all the trials and triumphs and changes, welcome and otherwise, the years had brought, he still loved her. He still saw her as his adoring bride.

"Now there's an example for our young couple," Henry observed. "Mac, why don't you share with Eggy what your wife has just reinforced with her actions?"

"Uh, okay," Mac shifted in his seat to face his more youthful counterpart. "My wife has just reinforced the age-old wisdom that every married man comes to understand—if you do as your wife tells you, you'll both be happy."

The room fell silent for only a split second before everyone broke into laughter.

"You should take notes," Kat said to Eggy, giving his hand a squeeze.

"All right then, this is the schedule: rotating lessons, lunch, then a relationship-building exercise—"

"Excuse me." Eggy's hand shot up. "A what?"

"Game," Mac translated.

Patsy pursed her lips as if to launch into a more complex explanation.

"Once you've been in on enough of these church retreat things like this you pick up the lingo." Mac gave Eggy an empathetic slap on the back. "All that means is they're going to have us make something or act out something or try to do something that will make us feel silly but in the end maybe reveal a little more about ourselves than we'd planned on showing."

Henry laughed and said, "I think that just about sums it up. Thank you, Mac."

"You're welcome." Mac then lowered his head and his voice as he told Eggy out of the corner of his mouth, "Don't worry about it, kid. Everyone here has your best interest at heart. And I give you my word. I won't let anyone make you do anything I wouldn't do myself."

"Looks like the male bonding has already begun," Louise said.

"Good. The last thing on the agenda for today, before our dinner, that is, will be the tests. Now we'll get down to work."

Chapter Seventeen

Alice glanced at the notes she had jotted on index cards and then at her watch. It was nearly four on Saturday afternoon, and she was standing in the waiting area at the conference with the other speakers who would make concluding remarks. She wondered if she should have gone with her first impulse and written out word for word what she wanted to say. Both Virginia and Mark had dismissed the idea.

"If you do that you will rely too heavily on getting every sentence said rather than getting your message across," Virginia had advised.

"Alice, I know you so well. You have so much to contribute, as much or more than anyone else sharing that panel with you today," Mark had said.

"But . . . ?" Alice gave him an encouraging look, knowing he had more he wanted to say.

"But you overthink things," Mark told her. "You want so much to do what is right and to please everyone that you sometimes lose sight of what you can do."

Alice could not argue. In fact, if she had allowed herself to take her usual course, she might well have thought herself right out of coming to this conference at all.

"Now, even if those other professionals start bandying about statistics, referencing pie charts or slides or whatever else to pretty up their presentations, don't let yourself get rattled," Virginia went on.

"You don't really think they will have charts and slides, do you?" Alice asked.

"It doesn't matter. My point is that the wisdom you have to share is every bit as valid and applicable as anything anyone else has to offer."

"What you have to share comes from a lifetime of experience," Mark added. "You also have a firm conviction in a better tomorrow. Right?"

"Right," she conceded to the fair description of her.

"Then share who you are, not just what you know," Mark continued. "You can't write that out and deliver it line by line. That has to come from your heart."

At the time they counseled her, their advice had sounded good. Alice had agreed and settled for sticking to an outline of high points and key phrases. Now, as she waited with the other special guest speakers behind the stage curtains for her introduction, she did wish she had the comfort of a fully composed address to fall back on.

She felt even more in need of a script when, at the last minute, Rachel asked the speakers to sign a waiver so that the presentation could be made available for "live streaming" on the Internet. Alice had understood early on that her likeness might be used, but the possibility of having people all over the world listen to what she had to say was a totally different matter. Well, she couldn't *not* sign, so she simply didn't allow herself to think about it.

Rachel walked by, saying something softly to each person she passed. When she reached Alice, she gave her hand a squeeze and said, "You'll dazzle them."

"Dazzle?" Alice whispered to herself nervously. Had she

ever in her whole life *dazzled* anyone? It seemed an awfully tall order.

Not too tall for you and the Lord to handle together, Alice told herself.

Rachel disappeared through the curtains.

The crowd settled down.

The speakers had been asked to gather behind the stage curtains early, so Alice had no idea if they had a huge audience or a small one. Mark and Virginia had both said the latest weather forecasts called for a cold snap, possibly on the heels of blustery winds that might cause some problems for travel. This gave Alice a small sliver of hope that many of the conference attendees had ducked away early to get home before the front moved in.

When Rachel introduced herself and thanked them all for making the conference so successful, the magnitude of the applause dashed Alice's hopes of having to face only a few stragglers. "I had no idea so many people would still be here," Alice said to no one in particular.

"They wouldn't be, usually," said a smartly dressed woman in heels so high that just looking at them made Alice feel off-kilter. The woman flicked back her long blonde hair to reveal her name badge with the subheading: Regional Vice President, Jewel/Evans Pharmaceutical Research and Development.

You have as much to contribute as anyone on the panel today. Alice tried to bolster her own confidence.

"There was talk of airport delays and flight cancellations. I heard a lot of people decided to stay the night and wait out the weather. So, we have a bigger crowd than even the planners expected," said the man in front of Alice. As he turned to talk to her, she could see that his badge listed his title as hospital administrator.

The fourth speaker, a doctor known for his pioneering

techniques in neurosurgery and for having written a best-seller giving advice on health, longevity and maintaining mental acuity, was nowhere in sight.

Rachel had explained to them as she double-checked the details for their introductions that the guest of honor would be brought in after the three of them had spoken. The planners would not require him to sit up on the stage through the opening presentations.

For that Alice felt truly grateful. She was nervous enough without imagining a quasicelebrity sitting behind her tapping his foot in anticipation of her summing up things so he could take center stage.

Center stage. Alice's heart rate picked up, thudding so hard in her ears that she didn't hear Rachel introduce her. The hospital administrator specialist whispered to her, "You're on!" and nudged her forward.

She stepped through the green velvet curtains, and there she was in front of her audience.

She gazed out at all the faces, or the ones she could see from the brightly lit platform. Many more people, she realized, filled the seats beyond the first two or three rows visible from her vantage point.

Alice acknowledged the group with a smile and a nod, and took her seat.

Rachel introduced the other two speakers and gave a quick overview of the conference. She praised all the people who had helped it become a reality. She had people step forward, mostly dedicated workers who stood along the side walls of the room. When the registration crew accepted recognition, Alice noticed Mark and Virginia standing nearby. Knowing where they were made Alice a little less anxious.

Then Rachel said, "I know many of you are eager to start home or to get to early dinner reservations or even just to get into more comfortable shoes."

A soft wave of laughter went through the group.

"So let's not wait another minute in getting on with the main event of the afternoon."

First was the vice president. She never seemed to stop moving as she talked. Her spike heels rat-tat-tatted across the wooden floorboards with the same clear and determined precision with which she delivered her predictions about the future of medicine. In her clear and well-documented calculations, that future lay in the many and nearly miraculous pharmaceutical advances already in the pipeline. She used sharp, decisive gestures.

The VP stated her case so convincingly that even Alice wondered, momentarily, if one day everything that ailed mankind could be dealt with by popping a pill.

Next came the hospital administrator. He opened with a joke about health-care providers going to heaven, which relaxed the crowd and dissipated any lingering electricity from the first speaker's dynamic presentation.

Then he got down to business and spoke of the harsh truths facing health care. He talked about health-care providers facing financial crises, staffing shortages and pressure to create change from politicians who did not understand the situation.

When he concluded, Alice got ready to make her simple presentation. *This has to come from your heart.* Again Mark's encouragement rang in her ears. Yes, Alice thought, what she had to share, after all, was not the kind of thing that could be captured in a pill or dictated by a politician.

With that thought and a quick prayer for presence of mind, she took the podium. She greeted the crowd, thanked Rachel, cleared her throat and began to share her message.

"Being back in Philadelphia, I have been reminded of my time here in nursing school. A wide-eyed daughter of a minister from cozy little Acorn Hill, Pennsylvania, I did not know if I would last a semester, much less complete the course. But

I had family, actually practically the whole *town*, praying for my success and believing in me even when I doubted myself. Those people played a large part in shaping the kind of nurse, the kind of person, I would become."

She looked out into the dimly lit room to the place where she had last seen Mark standing and found him smiling at her.

"You might think that is where my story, or any nurse's story, begins. But the truth is it goes back much further than that," she went on.

"I promise not to turn this short speech into a sermon, but I hope you will indulge me if I quote a passage from the Bible." She took a breath and then continued. "'For you created my inmost being; you knit me together in my mother's womb. I praise you because I am fearfully and wonderfully made; your works are wonderful, I know that full well'" (Psalm 139:13–14).

She paused to let them take that in. To her surprise she saw some people making notes and found that encouraging, not intimidating.

"I share that verse with you because even before I understood the concept of choosing one's life vocation, I knew I wanted to help people. My family might tell you I was born to do the kind of work I do."

It was a bold statement and she let it sink in a moment.

"In our modern terminology, those of you into research or up on the latest studies might stroke your chins and conclude that I was predisposed toward my chosen profession thanks to a newly found 'helper gene.' That my desire to help is in my DNA."

A murmur went through the crowd that told Alice she had captured their attention.

"I do not doubt this. I am the daughter of two of the greatest helpers I have ever known, my late father, Rev. Daniel Howard, and my mother, Madeleine, who passed away when I was still young. With the loss of our mother, my older sister and I had to step in and help raise the newborn daughter my mother left behind."

Alice glanced at her notes and realized she had departed from her outline and didn't know where to pick up again. She offered another quick prayer and tucked the notes away, along with her inhibitions.

"Even before then, though, I was the one whom people came to when they wanted a dolly's arm twisted back on or a stuffed animal patched up. Not because I was the best seamstress and certainly not because I was deft at figuring out how the various parts and pieces could be made whole again, but because even other children recognized in me that spark, that willingness to help. In short, they knew they had found someone who would do everything in her power to make it better no matter how hopeless things seemed."

The group laughed. They understood.

"I do not tell you this to extol my own virtues. I mention this in all humility because I feel I have come to nursing as a calling, not of my own doing but because it was always intended to be my purpose. Healing was and is my life's work, the duty I have been given in order to serve my fellow man."

Again she paused and a feeling of being in control spread over her.

"I hope that each of you who has dedicated yourself to the healing arts will see a bit of yourself in my description. This is my foundation—the desire to serve above all."

Alice searched the faces that she could see clearly and took comfort in their attentiveness to her words.

"Take a moment if you will and think about your own foundation, the moment you knew that healing and helping others would be your life's work."

The room grew still.

After a few seconds, Alice pressed on. "That spark, that

experience, that decision is what your work and life are built on, and that is where you must go to find what is cited in the title of this talk as your sense of *perspective*."

A woman in front scribbled hastily on a notepad in her lap.

"Begin there," Alice implored them, "but do not stop there."

She ventured a few feet from the podium.

"From that point, each and every one of us began to grow and learn. We committed ourselves to higher and higher forms of education, first in school and then in our fields—the lab, the hospital, the office, the home. Our ability to gain knowledge that we would apply again and again was not limited to classrooms or clinical settings. Nor should we ever assume we are finished with learning. Along the way we encounter disappointment and triumph, and both add to our frames of reference."

She took another step. It was not the forceful stride of the pharmaceutical representative, but for Alice it was like a leap of faith.

"The study of medicine is not a lightly taken pursuit. It requires of most of us not just time and dedication but that it join itself with who we are and change forever how we relate to the world. It often taxes our intellectual abilities. It tries our faith. It builds up our defenses and batters our emotions. It influences our worldview. It intrudes on our personal lives."

She returned to the podium. "Yes, medicine asks much of us. These are difficult times in our profession, times when we lack the resources to provide certain things for our patients. These are times when it is tempting simply to prescribe possible solutions to our patient's every ill. But medicine asks more of us than that. The moment you decided to answer your calling, you promised yourself more than that.

"I was asked to speak at this conference when the planner

learned that I had come in early to the hospital to check on a premature baby whose chance for survival was so precarious that his parents could not bring themselves to name him. I just got word this morning that the baby is going to go home from the hospital in a few days because of advances in medicine, creative efforts to get his needs paid for and the unflagging dedication of an entire staff of caring professionals."

The group broke into applause at that news. Alice fought not to get choked up. She quickly cleared her throat and continued. "There is a song we sing in church sometimes about the nature of giving—'I Will Not Offer That Which Costs Me Nothing.' Our work has meaning. It is reasonable it comes at times with a high price tag. If I were to ask each of you if the time and effort you dedicate to your profession is worth it, I hope you would answer *yes*."

Applause again.

"I know that much of what I've said seems obvious. But it also seemed woefully obvious to me that in the stressed-out, high-pressure world of charts and choices, with the threat of budget cuts and of malpractice suits looming over us, many of us have lost sight of the very reason we came to medicine. That is a shame because we were fearfully and wonderfully made for that service. With that as our foundation, our education and experience in our favor and all the amazing discoveries and advances being made every day, we all, every one of us, have the tools to give our best to those who look to us for help. Believe in your gifts and your hard-won victories, believe in yourself and go out and report for duty."

For a moment Alice stood there, stunned that she had gotten through her speech and said what she wanted to say. But how had it all been received? She smiled at the audience and said, "Thank you and I hope you all have a safe trip home."

Silence. Then the gathered group burst into applause, and Alice felt a flood of relief.

After the speeches had ended, many people, even the special guest speaker came up to her to tell her how much they liked and appreciated her remarks. She loved hearing that she had inspired people and given words to their own feelings, but it meant the most coming from her old friends Virginia and Mark.

"Well done!" Virginia gave her a hug.

"I knew you'd wow them," Mark added, planting a kiss on her cheek to congratulate her. "You've never let anyone down yet."

Alice wanted to protest his high praise but then decided that this had been the essence of her speech. She had been born to be someone people could count on, and she worked daily to live up to that calling. She was glad to do what she could at work, at home and even here.

Chapter Eighteen

A n inspirational reminder to us all,' that's what the famous doctor said."

Louise could envision Alice beaming as she described the praise given by the special guest speaker who had been listening to Alice's talk from the stage wings.

When Alice had called, she had caught her sister in the kitchen going through old sheet music. It had surprised Louise to discover how late it was, nearly a quarter after five in the evening.

"A bestselling author and medical pioneer." Alice reiterated the man's credentials. "Also, he is even more handsome in person than in his publicity photo. I'm so glad they didn't bring him out on the stage with the rest of us. I don't think I could have gotten out more than a few garbled words knowing he was sitting behind me."

"Oh, Alice, you would have done wonderfully under any circumstances."

"I appreciate your vote of confidence and your praying with me when I called home in a panic."

"Any time," Louise promised. "I'm only sorry I couldn't hear your talk. I hope Mark took plenty of pictures to share with us when you get back."

172 ✿ Annie Jones

"You don't have to wait *that* long," Alice said as if amused by the very idea of it.

"Why not?"

"Because it's on the Internet."

"You're going to send us the photos through e-mail?"

"E-mail? Um, I suppose I could do that, but I thought you'd just . . . Oh, didn't I tell you that part?"

"Apparently not," Louise chuckled at how Alice's success had made her usually quite sensible sister a bit scatterbrained.

"All conference attendees had to sign a waiver allowing the event-planning company and their designated agents— hospitals, hotels, wherever they might want to recruit speakers or to advertise—to use pictures and video of us in their materials and Web site."

"Web site?"

"Yes. According to Rachel, the video of the closing remarks of the conference is already on their site and probably, as a consequence, will pop up on video-sharing sites all over the world."

"How marvelous. The moment I have a break I'll try to find it."

"Louise, isn't it exciting what the Lord will do if you stay the course and serve Him instead of trying to serve your own version of what He wants for you?"

"Yes." Louise thought of the long day she had put in with the couples. "Though sometimes I wonder how we are to know the difference between the tasks the Lord has in mind for us and our own propensity for busywork."

"I understand." The very tone of Alice's voice confirmed that. "But I believe I have my answer. I didn't even want to take part in something that put me in front of more than a hundred people, and now my humble little speech can be accessed by millions around the world."

"I am so proud of you, Alice."

"And I'm a bit worried about you, Louise."

"Worried? Why?"

"That weariness in your voice. Your conjecture about how to tell the Lord's business from your own, what did you call it? A tendency toward . . . ?"

"Propensity for busywork," Louise repeated her choice of words.

"Is there anything I can do? Anything you want to share?"

"Thank you, Alice."

"Thank me? For what?"

"Because even though you are floating around on cloud nine after your memorable afternoon, you still listened to what I had to say and how I said it."

"*Can* I help?"

Louise mulled that over for a moment. "No, not really."

"Has something gone wrong?"

"There isn't anything wrong that I can put my finger on." Louise went over the day in her mind.

Though it had begun a bit awkwardly around the table, the prayer service and her reading from 1 Corinthians seemed to have a unifying effect on everyone. Then they all split up into separate rooms. The couples and Henry had spent the day immersed in classes, reading and tests.

Patsy had taken over the library to compile her scrapbook materials.

Mrs. Pennington had borrowed Eggy's laptop in order to update her blog.

Louise's contribution to the weekend seemed to consist of setting the two luncheon tables, following Jane's instructions for the preparation and presentation of the meal, and going from room to room at designated intervals to make sure everybody else kept to the schedule.

"The ladies' lunch went very nicely," she told Alice.

"Mrs. Pennington told us a funny story about how, for their sixtieth anniversary, her husband tried to fit into his uniform from his days in the Navy during World War II.

"It seemed that he tried to do something special every year, something to take her back to the day he first saw her or to their wedding day, I wasn't quite clear which it was."

"Very romantic."

"Yes. In fact, in talking to the group I remembered a time in Philadelphia when I played their song for them. I had a chance to go through my files and find that old sheet music after lunch. I plan to play it for her before she goes."

"That doesn't sound like busywork to me. That sounds like a task with a very worthy purpose."

"Yes, except that I lost all track of time and forgot to signal the end of the lengthiest of the tests taken this afternoon." Louise still felt her cheeks flush at having made such a slip up. "Luckily I had Mrs. Pennington there to come to my aid."

"By alerting them to the time herself?"

"No, by announcing to them that trying to keep to such a tight schedule as a means of forming bonds with each other was poppycock." That opinion was, Louise supposed, at the very crux of her malaise. Though she wouldn't deem their efforts poppycock, she wondered about their approach to the weekend. If the goal was to help create a foundation for Eggy and Kat, how was anything going on in the inn today really accomplishing that? How could Louise be of more service toward making that goal a reality? She just didn't see herself as vital to the goings-on in any way.

"Poppycock," Alice murmured.

"*Hmm?*"

"I can practically hear your brain churning, Louise," Alice said. "You know what that means?"

"Please tell me."

"What that means," Alice told her, "is that you are over-thinking things."

"Overthinking? Is there such a thing?"

"There is. If you doubt it for one moment, just ask Mrs. Pennington."

"I think I'll pass on that option," Louise graciously conceded Alice's point. "But what does one do to avoid the problem of overthinking?"

"You do what I did today."

"Make a speech?"

"Say a prayer, trust yourself and the Lord, take some time to get perspective and then let the rest come from your heart."

"I can do that," Louise assured her sister. "In fact, we began this undertaking with prayer and I've shared the Lord's Prayer with you today, so I'm on track with that so far."

"Good."

"I like what you suggest about finding perspective." Louise took a moment to look at where she was, holing up in the kitchen, trying both to avoid everyone and to look out for their needs. "I think perhaps I will spend some time alone in my room, reading the Bible and maybe a little C. S. Lewis."

"You go and do that, then. I don't want to keep you from having some quiet time." Alice held the phone away and said something to someone in the distance. "Sorry about that. Virginia and Mark are hashing out where they want to pick up takeout. Then we're heading to Mrs. Pennington's for dinner, and then, after Mark heads home, we girls plan to relax and watch TV all snug and cozy."

"I'll let you go then. We'll have plenty of time to discuss it tomorrow on the car trip home."

"If we can *make* the car trip home tomorrow."

"Make it? Why wouldn't we?"

"Haven't you been keeping up with the weather?"

"Last I heard was first thing this morning when they called for the misty rain to change over to snow, which it did around noon. Temperatures expected to stay cold but seasonal. Then, late tonight . . ."

A click on the line told Louise someone was trying to get a call through to the inn.

"Jane was going to call," she mused aloud.

"I'm sorry? Jane?"

"She was going to call before she came back to make the meal. I bet she has a question. I hate doing this but I'd better say good-bye to you and take that call."

"Give her my love and we'll talk tomorrow."

Louise got off the line with one sister and moments later found herself connected to her other sister.

"Well, I guess you know why I'm calling," Jane skipped over the usual pleasantries and got to the point as soon as Louise answered.

"I assume you want to make sure we don't need you to pick up anything before you come home."

"Pick up? Louise, you don't expect me to come back to the inn now, do you?"

"Expect it?" She got up from the table where she had been sitting, facing the hallway so that she could see and hear if someone needed her. "I am counting on it and so are the seven hungry people in this house anticipating that we will all start cooking a meal together in twenty minutes."

"Twenty minutes? Is it that late already? I am so sorry I didn't call you sooner, but I lay down to let my mud mask and the cucumbers on my eyes do their work and I fell asleep. I had no idea it was so late."

Mud? Cucumbers? "Where are you?"

"At Sylvia's."

"You did bring the groceries by earlier, though, didn't you?"

"Yes. They're all where you'd expect to find them."

Louise turned toward the kitchen, wondering if she could get the couples started while they waited for Jane. "If you tell me where to find the recipes you earmarked, I'll get things ready. Don't worry, just hurry and get here as fast as you can and we'll—"

"Hurry? Get there? Louise, don't you understand? I'm not coming."

Louise felt as though a lead weight had dropped into the pit of her stomach. The time she had spent going through boxes of old sheet music had left her mind dull. "Did you say you're *not coming*?"

"I may have learned to drive in the Pennsylvania winters but I spent far too much time in San Francisco to have the kind of skills I'd need to navigate in this stuff."

"This what? A little snow?" It suddenly dawned on Louise that she hadn't even looked outside since lunchtime when they had all admired the fat, fluffy snowflakes. She turned toward the kitchen door, talking to Jane as she did. "Really, Jane, it's not as if I'm asking you to trek through the Yukon. Just a short trip braving the minor inconvenience of a little . . ."

Louise stared out at the mess that greeted her through the open door, beyond the back porch. A frigid blast of wind whisked tiny droplets of ice into her hair, onto her sweater and stung her warm cheek.

Louise finished her assessment of Jane's situation in a voice so meek it hardly rated as anything more than a whispered squeak, ". . . snow."

"Looked outside, did you?"

"Yes." Louise scanned the scene before her.

Snow did not faze her, nor did brutal cold, nor wind nor, well, any of the things noted in the postman's code. Like that trusty delivery person, none of those things would normally keep Louise from carrying out her appointed rounds. But this? "It's . . ."

"Ice."

The familiar landscape now looked encased in a thick layer of glasslike ice. The bushes and tree branches bowed and slowly swayed under its weight. Icicles hung from the roof.

The "dusting" of snow that Louise had expected looked more like a gleaming silver blanket over grass, vehicles, every flat surface. It swathed everything in frozen silence.

Nothing moved. No one was out and about. There wasn't even the distant sound of a car to break the quiet.

"I was going to say it's beautiful," Louise observed. "But, yes, it is ice. Pure ice."

"The mist we had all morning was the culprit. Soaked everything. They couldn't pretreat the roads because the chemicals would have just washed away. Then the cold moved in so quickly, there was nothing to be done."

"How do you know all this?"

"I spent the morning running errands around town, remember? Seems as though everyone had an opinion on what the weather would do next. Aunt Ethel and I talked it over and sided with the people who thought that it might get a bit blustery but not really bad, so we forged ahead with our spa plans."

Louise shut the door and even as she did, one last swirl of icy precipitation whipped around her feet.

"Thank you for keeping her company today. She'd be welcome, of course, but I have to say I do appreciate having one fewer person to cater to around here."

As is often the way when one says something that might easily be misconstrued, it seemed that every person in the inn picked that time to converge around Louise.

She quickly got some cooking instructions from Jane,

and then said, "Thanks, Jane. The group has just come in to start dinner. I'll explain the situation. Good-bye."

"What's up?" Eggy asked, his wife two steps behind him.

"Is there anything I can do to help?" Kat asked.

"Have you looked outside?" Maggie was only a few foot-falls behind Kat.

"Isn't it dinnertime?" Mac wondered aloud.

"Henry has chased me out of the office so he can go over the test material and compile some figures for the after-dinner session," Patsy announced.

The group gave a collective groan.

"I thought we'd finished up with all that," Mac protested.

"We have!" Patsy held up her hands as if to say "ta-da," your wish is granted. Then she slapped those hands together and said, "Until after dinner when we go over the results."

More groans from the group.

"Looks like the little groundhogs have stuck their heads out of their holes in time to see that it's really winter." Agnes came slowly down the stairs, chuckling at her own observation.

And once again Louise found herself seeing Agnes' somewhat skewed viewpoint. The bleary-eyed group did appear aimless, slightly confused.

Patsy clapped her hands again. "So why don't we just get started preparing the meal we planned?"

Chapter Nineteen

Louise began to arrange the ingredients for the meal. In one area of the counter, she set out flour, oil, salt, eggs and olive oil. Then she went into the pantry to retrieve Jane's pasta machine.

Next, she got packages of ground chuck and mild Italian sausage from the refrigerator and placed them near the stove top, where she had already laid out a heavy frying pan and cover. She set up another cooking station on the other side of the stove top. There she arranged jars of tomatoes and tomato sauce that Jane had put up last fall, a tube of tomato paste, some cloves of garlic and fresh basil and oregano.

Last, she took out several kinds of greens, green and red peppers, large mushrooms, and a red onion and set these by the sink.

The group watched her actions hungrily.

"All right," she said. "We're set to begin. Jane thought the men might like to try their hands at making the sauce. The women will divide into pasta makers, salad makers and meat cookers."

"*Ohhh*," said Kat, "I'd love to try making the pasta if someone will help me. I got a pasta machine for a wedding present and have no idea how to use it."

"It's a cinch," said Maggie, "I'll have you grinding out the lasagna noodles like you've been doing it all your life."

Kat looked absolutely delighted. "I had no idea when we voted on lasagna that we'd be making it from scratch."

"My dear," Louise said, "when you cook with Jane, or in this case without her but with her preparations, you do everything the 'right' way."

"Oh, this is going to be fun!" Patsy exclaimed. "I'll make the salad, if that's okay with you and Agnes."

"That's fine with me, dear," Agnes said. "Salad making is one of my least favorite tasks. In fact, I usually only have salads when I eat out. At home, I'll nibble on a carrot or pile some lettuce on my sandwich to get my veggies."

"Yes, that's fine with me too," Louise told her. "I'll just cook the beef and the sausage and have them ready with the cheeses for when we layer the lasagna. Agnes, perhaps you could be the sous-chef and help out where needed."

"Wonderful. As you know, I'm very good at giving advice . . . and orders, for that matter."

Everyone laughed, and a happy atmosphere enveloped the kitchen as the group began the preliminaries for their meal.

It had gotten dark outside even before they started the food preparation. The wind had picked up. It howled around the corners of the old home and whistled through the branches of the trees nearby. From time to time it rattled the windows or peppered the door and windows with sprays of icy pellets. The wildness of the weather added to the sense of coziness shared by Louise and the other occupants of Grace Chapel Inn that night.

The men, with some instruction from Agnes, began by chopping garlic and herbs and then adding them to some olive oil that they had warmed in a pan. When the garlic and herbs had released their flavors into the oil, Eggy carefully added the tomatoes, tomato sauce and some of the paste. He brought the sauce to a simmer and lowered the heat a bit so that it would cook slowly.

"I do apologize that the sauce isn't being made quite the way Jane would have liked," Louise said. "She was going to get it started in the early afternoon so it could cook for several hours, but the weather intervened. However, I'm sure it will taste wonderful, now that we have our capable chefs working on it."

"*Humph*," Mac said, taking mock affront, "Our efforts will be superb. You are lucky. Henry, Eggy and I don't mind working for our supper. Now singing for our supper is an entirely different matter."

"Heaven forbid," Maggie said with a laugh. "We'd like to keep our appetites, thank you."

Another burst of laughter was interrupted by a squeal from Kat. "Oh, I did it!" she cried exuberantly. "Look, a real lasagna noodle!"

She and Maggie had mixed the egg, flour, salt, oil and water into a stiff dough and then had kneaded it. Then they had fed the dough into the pasta machine to roll it to the correct thinness. After that Kat had threaded the dough back into the machine, set it to make lasagna noodles, and the machine rolled out a wavy-edged strip of pasta.

Everyone gathered around Kat's work of culinary art and applauded.

Patsy exclaimed, "Oh, this is so much fun. I think—"

Crack! A terrifying sound, a burst of light and then total darkness interrupted Patsy's words.

"Oh my goodness! What's happened to the lights?" Patsy said, voicing what they all were thinking.

Even in the darkness, Louise could feel them looking to her for answers.

"Well, a safe guess is that the ice has brought down some power lines." Louise would have felt silly stating the obvious except that the group seemed to need to hear it. "As you know, ice storms happen from time to time around here, but we have provisions for just such an emergency."

"Those provisions don't include a backup generator, do they?" Mac asked.

"No. I'm afraid that hasn't been in our budget. But we do have a store of candles, oil lamps, that kind of thing. And the house is well insulated, so as long as we don't open the doors, we'll be comfortable for several hours. If you all will just stay where you are, I'll go get something to shed a little light on our situation."

"I'll use my cell phone to call the electric company and report the p-problem," Henry said.

In short order Louise came back into the room, her way lit by a glass oil lamp. In the pockets of her cardigan, she had slipped a handful of white emergency candles and tucked under her arm was a large emergency flashlight. Working together, the group quickly had the kitchen flooded with warm, glowing light.

"The p-power company says the, uh, uh, the outage is widespread," Henry came back into the kitchen from the front hall where he had found the best signal. "Tree limbs have fallen on electrical wires in spots all over town. They are asking people to stay in their homes, even if they feel they can manage to drive on the ice, b-b-because of the danger of coming in contact with a . . . with a d-downed wire."

Somebody's stomach growled. And Kat said in a little voice, "I guess our lasagna dinner is canceled."

Mac nodded. "I have my truck. How about we phone Zachary's and place an order for me to go pick up and bring back."

"Mac, sweetheart, even if the restaurant is open, which I doubt, that would take you the better part of the evening just to navigate the roads, let alone the danger from downed lines."

"In other words . . . ?" he asked.

"In other words you are staying right here."

Mac opened his mouth, possibly to launch a counter argument, but Eggy stepped up and slapped his mentor-in-training on the back. "Give it up, buddy. A wise man once told me that if you do as your wife asks, you both stay happy."

"Can't dispute that sound advice." Mac laughed.

"C'mon, don't worry. Some of the best meals Kat and I ever have are at the end of the month when we're low on funds and we have to make do with what's left in the cupboard and fridge. We just throw it all together, add salt, garlic, pepper, whatever we have. It's called . . . what *is* it called?"

"Being young?" Mac shook his head.

"Improvising?" Louise suggested.

"Yeah." Eggy snapped his fingers. "Improvising. Like jazz. You bring what you know how to do, and I bring what I know how to do, and together we create something better than either of us could have done alone."

Louise nodded her head in appreciation of that simple but thought-provoking example. "Henry, I think Edgar just summed up what I had hoped we would accomplish this weekend."

Henry cast a sad-eyed gaze toward the office and all those tests. Then he nodded his head and smiled.

"Well, all isn't lost, thanks to Jane's insistence on a gas cook top," Louise said. "The electric starter won't work, but all we have to do is light a match and turn the burner on."

"That's terrific," Patsy said. "I have an all-electric kitchen, which I love, but it's not great when the power fails."

"Okay, so let's decide what we can improvise from the ingredients we have," Kat suggested.

"Well, as you said, the lasagna is out because the oven is electric. However, the sauce and the meats are already cooked. The salad is fine. I suggest we cook some of the dried spaghetti or pasta that we have in the pantry and perhaps we can warm the bread on the cover of the pot in which we'll boil the water."

"Great idea," said Eggy. "If you have some ziti or rigatoni, we can even use the ricotta. Kat and I are usually too rushed to make lasagna, so we mix the cheese and meat in with the cooked pasta and then pour the sauce over that. It's pretty good."

"That sounds wonderful," Maggie said. "I might just try that at home when I don't have a lot of time."

In a matter of minutes, lively chatter again filled the warm kitchen.

"Put in some mozzarella with the ricotta and the hot pasta," Mac offered.

"Hey, that's a good idea. We haven't tried that," Eggy said as he added the grated cheese. It melted with the heat of the ziti.

Patsy dressed the salad with homemade balsamic vinaigrette and sprinkled on some freshly grated parmesan.

Agnes used the blue placemats and blue-and-white checked napkins that Jane had left on the buffet for setting the dining table. In the middle of the table, she placed Jane's centerpiece, an arrangement of artichokes, small eggplants and red peppers in a colorful Italian pottery bowl. Two hurricane globes over fat red candles completed the picture.

"Okay, ladies, the main course is hot, delicious and ready to be served," Mac announced.

"We're all set," Patsy said. "The bread and salad are on the table."

"I'm almost done f-filling the water glasses," Henry announced as Eggy carried the large serving dish into the dining room and set it on the hot pad that Louise had provided.

They all took their places and joined hands while Henry offered grace.

"Dear Father, thank You for this food and for this fellowship. Use it and us according to Your will. Watch over everyone in p-peril tonight from this storm, and everyone in peril every day from the many unseen storms that come against them. We p-pray that they would come to know You as the one constant Who will always stand with them against the tempest." He fell silent and then another voice rose.

"Thank You for bringing together these people who have given so kindly of their time to help each other and our church," Patsy said.

Another brief silence and then Maggie spoke, "Bless this gathering not just as we break bread and share this last night in the inn together but also go with us as we return to our everyday lives."

"And remind us not to get so comfortable in those everyday lives that we resist the chances You put before us to learn and grow and help others do the same," Mac added.

"Thank You for these people who, even though they do not know us well, have shown they love us in Your name," Kat murmured.

"Thank You for the shelter of this awesome place, the roof, the walls, the warmth from the candles and from the hearts of Louise Howard and her sisters," Eggy spoke up to make himself heard above a swell of wind banging against the windows.

"Thank You for the wonderful life You have given me. Thank You for the new friendships we have made and the old ones we have renewed," Agnes managed in a voice thinned by emotion.

Her aged hand gave Louise's a squeeze.

Louise drew in the aroma of the wonderful food. Eyes shut, she could not shut out the glow of light surrounding them. In the hands held in hers and the words spoken in her home, she felt the connection she knew this weekend was meant to provide for all of them.

She cleared her throat and spoke as Alice had asked her, from her heart, "Thank You for the gift of improvisation as well as the aptitude for organization and for bringing them both together for Your greater good tonight. Thank You for the opportunity to serve You with our talents, with our hopes and with our willing hands."

"Amen," Henry concluded.

"Amen," the rest responded together.

The meal was delicious, and everyone was enthusiastic about Kat and Eggy's pasta invention. Conversation was lighthearted and easy. Although the testing had kept them separate for most of the day, the camaraderie created in the kitchen over cooking chores was evident.

As they finished the Italian cheesecake that Maggie had brought from home the day before, the wind picked up again and the whole house shook.

Cra-a-ack.

It was like the sound they heard just before the lights went out, but this time it was followed by the sound of breaking glass.

Chapter Twenty

The frozen tree limb that had come crashing down had not only broken a window in the sunroom, but it had also broken the bond the group had finally forged.

The women busied themselves sweeping up all the shards of glass while the men used an old card table to board up the window. Henry called the power company again to learn that they did not think they would have things up and running in the Grace Chapel Inn area for a few more hours.

They all returned to the dining room to clear the dishes into the kitchen. They rinsed their dishes and stacked them in the dishwasher, awaiting the return of the power. They tidied up the kitchen, and when they were finished, stood around the oil lamp on the kitchen table, awkwardly attempting to make small talk.

"Maybe we should just try to get some sleep," Maggie said.

Louise's spirits slumped. If they retired, the weekend was as good as over. Tomorrow morning, weather permitting, they would eat breakfast and go off to church. They might share a pew during services, but afterward everyone would go his or her own way. Louise, Jane and Agnes Pennington would have to leave to meet Alice and Virginia as planned. If they wanted to make Making Marriage Matter work, they could not walk away from it now.

"We did have a session planned to discuss p-preliminary findings of some of the tests," Henry said. "B-but I can't go over those tests in the dark. Also, the information a-a-about the tests is on my laptop, which is out of b-battery power."

"Mine is too," Eggy grumbled. "Mrs. P. had just plugged it in to recharge before we started dinner. It wouldn't have built up much run time before the lights cut off."

Louise straightened her shoulders. "We do not require a laptop or a program or even electricity to interact with one another," she reminded them.

"B-but our goal this weekend was more than merely entertaining ourselves. We came here to learn about our young people and figure out how to b-best help them."

"Then why don't you just ask them how you can help them?" Agnes shook her head. "Lands, I'm beginning to wonder what you folks would have done if I had stayed in Philly this weekend."

"Ask them?" Patsy seemed perplexed by the notion.

"Ask them," Louise reiterated Agnes advice. "Only not here. Let's go into the parlor. Mac and Henry and Eggy, you can start a fire in the fireplace. Kat, please carry the lamp in to light the way for Mrs. Pennington. Patsy and I will gather some blankets to keep the chill off until the fire gets going."

"What shall I do?" Maggie asked.

"Why don't you rearrange the chairs so that they are all near the fire?"

Within fifteen minutes the fire had begun to pop and crackle. Everyone had taken seats. Maggie had pushed chairs to form a circle. Kat and Eggy had opted to sit on the floor near the fireplace.

The whole scene reminded Louise of the reason they had put the Christmas tree in the room this past season. They had hoped it would bring their friends and family close together in an atmosphere of love and security. Tonight they didn't need the holiday trappings. They only needed to be open to Christ's love and to one another.

"I'm n-not sure exactly how to lead this off." Henry rubbed his hands together. "There wasn't an article or study or program for just . . . just . . . just talking."

Mac gave an empathetic laugh. "See, honey? I'm not the only guy around who likes to rely on the tried and true."

"Yes and y-you m-might, might guess that just . . . just talking is n-not m-my strong suit. Th-those of you who know m-me understand I'm . . . I'm m-more of an . . . of an administrator."

"And an excellent listener," Patsy chimed in. "He'd have to be, of course, with a chatterbox like me for a wife."

Henry laughed gently and nodded his head. The golden light from the fire reflected off the rim of his glasses and gave his white hair a blondish cast.

Louise wondered if that's how he looked when he was a young man. She smiled. She realized that Patsy still saw him as though he were fresh out of seminary and their lives together just beginning, not unlike the way that Kat looked at Eggy.

Louise wondered if the young redhead would still gaze at her husband with such affection many years from now. She hoped it would be so and knew that what they all did tonight might well be a means of making sure it did.

"Then maybe we should do as Agnes suggested," Louise said. "Let's ask Kat and Eggy to tell us how they think our church and those of us here tonight can help them keep their marriage a top priority."

"Excellent, Louise." Even in the play of dark and light around the room, the relief Henry felt shone brightly on his face. "What can we do for you?"

Eggy looked at Kat.

Kat looked at Eggy.

"Well . . ." Kat looked at her hands in her lap.

"We signed up for this mostly hoping . . ." She looked at her husband and whispered, "You say it."

Eggy shrugged. "We just wanted friends."

"Friends?" Maggie said it as though she couldn't understand anyone needing to sign up for anything to find friendship.

"Then you got matched to the right mentor couple. Maggie here makes friends everywhere she goes." Mac put his hand on his wife's shoulder. "You didn't have to give up your whole weekend for that."

Maggie looked back over that shoulder at her husband.

"Not that it hasn't been worth it," Mac hastened to add.

"But . . . um . . . you see . . . we were talking about this during our free time today." Eggy ran his hand back through his dark hair.

Kat smoothed the wake of dark waves where his fingers had mussed it and, her eyes locked with his, said, "The thing is, we are not sure it *has* been worth it."

"N-no?"

Patsy leaned in, waiting for the young couple to say more. Mac and Maggie did the same. Louise did as well.

Agnes remained relaxed, almost as if she fully expected this to come out when she had first suggested posing a simple question to the test couple.

"No." Eggy placed one foot flat on the floor, bent his leg and rested his forearm across his knee.

"Not that you haven't all been totally super," Kat rushed to say.

"And the food was great," Eggy threw in.

"But?" Louise prodded.

"But . . ." Kat shifted her gaze to the now roaring fire. "But we feel like . . ."

"Can I ask you a question?" Eggy made a circular motion with his finger to show that "you" meant the whole committee.

"Anything." Henry held his hands open.

Eggy looked to his wife for support and then to the members of the committee. "Why us?"

"You signed up for this," Patsy said sounding bewildered.

"Yeah, but so did some other people, right?" Eggy looked to Henry for confirmation.

"Two other couples, yes."

"So, why us?" Eggy repeated and then held up his hand to hold off anyone answering until he had made his point. "And don't tell me it's because we're young. We know that. Maybe the statistics on young marriages aren't that great, but it couldn't just be an age thing."

Louise thought of the young couple close to Kat and Eggy's age that she had specifically lobbied against including in their beginning effort. She met Eggy's eyes with a look that urged him to continue with his thoughts.

"There *is* more to it. We, Kat and I, we sort of feel that whatever it was that made you want us for the program might actually be the thing that will keep us from getting what we *need* from the program."

"We chose you because you seemed the ones *most* in need of outside support," Patsy explained.

"Listen to that. The way you chose to say it shows exactly what I'm saying. You picked us because you found us the neediest as opposed to picking us because you thought we had the most potential."

The room went still except for the crackle of the fire and the ever-present howl of the wind beyond the walls.

"You picked us . . ." Eggy went on, ". . . because you thought our problems suited your solutions."

In that instant Eggy's distinction brought Louise full circle back to the concept of making oneself ready to do whatever the Lord asks. She had surrendered herself to be used in the way the Lord needed her but then set about looking for ways to serve that made the most sense to *her*. That gave her the chance to use what she felt were her gifts. She had done the right thing, but not for all the right reasons.

"It's a subtle thing," Kat admitted. "But it makes us feel that you don't really have faith in our marriage."

"What?" Maggie shook her head. "No."

"How could you say that?" Patsy sounded genuinely hurt.

"Because you tested us instead of talking to us. You set out from the start looking for what was wrong with us and our marriage."

"But you told us those things yourselves. The red flags were right there on your application," Patsy argued.

"I know this project m-means a lot to you, Patsy, but please, let me handle it from here." Henry placed his hand on her shoulder, and then fixed his gaze on the couple seated by the fire. "I am sorry you t-two feel this way."

"Red flags? We had *red flags* on our application?" Kat asked, obviously upset.

"Th-the other couples had support systems of some kind in p-place. You didn't. The others had statistics on their side."

"We didn't," Eggy acknowledged.

"The other p-people had a shared history."

"What does that mean?" Eggy asked

"They knew each other very well b-before they even considered marriage."

"We knew each other," Kat insisted.

"Oh? We didn't realize . . ." Louise looked to Henry who gave her a nod to encourage her to finish her thought. "On your application you said you met on the Internet and married after less than a year, having only met in person a few times."

"*That* is a red flag," Patsy said quietly.

"Poppycock!"

Louise shut her eyes. *Not now, Agnes*, she wanted to say but she held her tongue.

"Now I am not a member of your church, so you may

think that when it's time to bail out the boat my bucket won't hold any water."

They all looked at her.

"That won't prevent me from trying to keep this ship afloat." Agnes gave a sharp nod of her head. "I've seen and done a lot in my more than eighty years on God's green earth, and the one thing I know for sure is that I don't know nearly enough. And I never will." She slapped her own leg for emphasis. "That doesn't keep me from trying to learn as much as I can for as long as I am able."

Louise liked that message. She was glad she hadn't tried to quell her old neighbor's outburst.

"To do that, to always keep learning, means you have to keep an open mind," Agnes went on. "I wonder how this weekend might have gone differently if you had done that. If everyone in this room who wanted to make your church program a success had entered into the project thinking that you all had a lot to learn, that you all needed to both give and get support from one another."

"But we already have so much support and help and years of experience." Maggie made a sweeping gesture to include the Leys, Louise and herself and Mac.

"We were looking at it the way you helped me, Agnes. When Eliot and I were first married and I didn't have a mother to turn to for advice, remember?" Louise thought of the sheet music she had searched out earlier today. "You and Woodrow had such a wonderful relationship. You kept your love strong, your romance alive for so long."

"Woody and I?" Agnes laughed so softly it seemed an amusement for her benefit alone. "You're trying to tell me that you picture me and my Woodrow akin to the older couples in this room, the ones who have all the answers, the ones who began their marriage without all those pesky red flags?"

"Yes." Louise *had* thought that. Now she found herself beginning to wonder what she might have missed.

"Oh, my dear, if you only knew."

"Knew what?"

"I, the former Agnes Cecelia Beasley, married Woodrow Wilson Pennington on July 15th, 1945—the very first day I ever laid eyes on him."

"Wow. This evening suddenly took an interesting turn," Kat murmured, scooting a little close to where Agnes was seated.

"Really?" Louise tried to remember if she had ever heard such a claim from Agnes before. "All these years I've known you, you've never so much as hinted at that."

"Didn't I?" Agnes cocked her head. "That just goes to show you that you probably don't know anyone as well as you assume you do."

"That's incredible. You married your husband on the day you met him?"

"No. Now I didn't say that." She held up her hands and her slim golden wedding band winked in the dancing fire light. "I said I married him on the same day I first laid eyes on him. On that day, I knew that man as well or better than most couples of my acquaintance then, or now, knew each other on their wedding day."

She took a good long look at everyone.

Louise shifted in her seat, partly from wanting to hunker down and enjoy listening to her old friend and partly from feeling a bit unsettled by the barebones honesty of the older woman's penetrating gaze.

"You see, I had actually known Woody Pennington for almost three years before that sunny day in July when I became his bride."

"But you'd never *seen* him?" Patsy wrinkled up her nose like someone trying to fit all the pieces of a puzzle together and not quite getting it.

"Not in person, no. I had a photo of him. Small, black and white and faded with time. Still, it was good enough that

I could pick him out of a thousand other sailors disembarking that day."

"A thousand other sailors?" Patsy couldn't make heads or tails of Agnes story. "But you recognized him?"

"Because I *knew* him. Not just his face or his build, though I had spent enough time staring at that old photo to have committed those to memory." Agnes looked up and away as if she could see the old picture in her mind's eye. "No, it was more than just how he looked. I knew him because he had revealed himself to me, heart and soul."

Patsy shook her head. "How?"

"In his letters, dear." The sweetest, saddest expression lit Agnes' age-etched face. "We wrote letters."

Kat turned to Eggy. "Like you and me."

"Yeah." He grinned and nodded. "Only ours were instant messages and e-mail."

"Yes. Woody and I were once very much like our young Kat and Eggy, as all young people in love are. We were also as different from these two as the world is different now."

Eggy lifted his head to look at her with open curiosity. "You mean because when you were our age the whole world was at war?"

Agnes nodded. "Love hasn't changed. All the world over and all throughout time, there are wars and rumors of wars, as the Bible promises. There are good times and bad, bleakness and joy. Still, love is a constant."

"A kiss is still a kiss," Louise borrowed a phrase from "As Time Goes By."

"A sigh is just a sigh," Maggie sang softly.

Without prompting the group began to sing softly together the old song that reminded people of the very thing that Agnes had been talking about.

Louise got up and moved to the piano and played along.

When the last note had faded she turned around on the piano bench to see Agnes wiping away a tear. Louise had to slip out the handkerchief she kept tucked in her pocket and do likewise.

"Thank you," Agnes said. "Thank you all for that."

"Now you have to tell us the rest of the story," Maggie urged.

"How did you start writing letters to someone you didn't know?" Mac wanted to know.

"How did you finally meet?" Kat jumped in, pressing her hand on her husband's cheek as she asked, "Was it love at first sight?"

"All right. All right." Agnes put her hand over her heart and laughed. "I'll tell you the whole story. Let's see. It began my senior year in high school when our home-economics teacher gave us the assignment to write a letter a week to be sent to a soldier in a battle zone."

"Your teacher had you write to strange men?" Patsy wondered about that.

"We were at war. We were doing our duty to keep morale up. These were *our* boys." Agnes took a deep breath. "We did not think of them as strangers, we thought of them as heroes."

The whole group seemed to move in closer, mesmerized by that thought.

"There wasn't a one of us who did not know some young man off at war, some family with a gold star in the window."

"A gold star?" Eggy asked for clarification.

"There were small cardboard flags. A white star meant you had a member of your family serving. Gold meant they had paid the ultimate sacrifice."

A respectful silence fell over them for a moment.

"So we girls did what we could. We wrote nice, chatty letters talking about the most ordinary things. We hoped it made a difference, if only for a little while," Agnes went on. "I got several lovely notes back, and for the duration of my senior year I kept up with those fellows through the mail."

"And one of them was your future husband?" Patsy tried to push things along, her eyes glittering with anticipation for more of the story.

"Yes." Agnes nodded. "Woodrow was the only one of the bunch that I continued to write to after graduation."

"Why him?" Kat asked.

"Why Eggy, my dear?" Agnes smiled slowly. "You must have come across all sorts of nice fellows online."

"And some not so nice," Eggy muttered.

"More of the not-nice kind," Kat agreed.

"So what was it about our Edgar Wickham that captured your imagination? What made your heart skip when the little icon appeared to announce that you had mail and you saw it was from him?"

"He had perfect spelling," Kat whispered.

"What?" Eggy asked, clearly bemused.

"You didn't try to impress me with abbreviations and text talk. You were just yourself." She kissed his cheek.

Louise didn't know if the young man blushed or if it was a trick of the firelight.

Still, the sweetness of the moment gave her courage to confess something she rarely told anyone—"Eliot could take almost any song and belt it out on the piano in a rip-roaring boogie-woogie arrangement without a note of music in front of him."

Everyone turned to Louise in astonishment.

Louise had surprised herself a little in sharing that. "Very few people knew that about him. When he did it for me, I knew there was so much more to him than the staid professor-of-music persona he showed everyone else."

It grew quiet for a moment when finally Maggie giggled and blurted out, "Mac looked cute in a paper hat."

"Do not go there," Mac warned.

"Too late." She ruffled her hand through his sandy-brown hair. "His cousin was a friend of mine who thought we'd be perfect for each other. She took me by the burger joint where Mac worked, and we never dated anyone else after that."

"If I had taken a job in a pizza parlor instead, who knows who'd be sitting here instead of me," Mac joked.

"When I first heard Henry preach," Patsy volunteered at last, "it was . . ." She looked to the man at her side and bit her lower lip.

With a nod, he gave her permission to say the rest.

She faced them all. "It was the most painful thing I had ever witnessed." Tears flooded her eyes. Her lip quivered. Her voice went high and raspy as she concluded, "And the bravest."

Louise had seldom been so grateful for her ever-ready cloth hankie.

"There, you see, it's never the same thing and it's always the same thing. Why Woody? Because like Eggy and Eliot and Mac and Henry, he revealed his true self to me and it was exactly whom I had always hoped he would be."

Kat sniffled.

"For me that came after I wrote a letter in which I told him that if I ever wrote too much or if he found my news from home irrelevant and childish to just let me know and I'd stop." Agnes wiped away another tear. "And in his next letter he told me that my letters were one of the only things in his life that did not feel irrelevant. That my news of home often gave him the only peace and hope he had in an entire day."

"Oh my. We have no idea what those men suffered," Louise said.

"What all soldiers have suffered," Eggy reminded them that war was not the provenance of the older generations alone.

"For the first time he signed his letter, 'With all my love, Woody.'"

The ladies sighed so perfectly in unison that it was as if they had been directed to do so by an unseen choir master.

Mac and Henry chuckled.

"I wrote him back immediately, of course, telling him I felt the same way. But I couldn't bring myself to send the letter."

"It's scary." Kat unfolded her slender legs and leaned back on her palms. "Big step."

"I thought so as well," Agnes said. "Then we began hearing about something we could never have imagined— the kamikazes. And soon after that a gold star went up in the house across the street."

"Oh no," Louise found herself saying as if she might have known the family personally.

"I did not hesitate. I sent that letter and one every day after. I never once withheld my feelings from Woody from that point on." Agnes slashed her hand through the air to underscore her steadfastness in that. "He told me later that those two weeks when I didn't send a letter were the longest of his life, and not because of the war."

"*Ooh*, poor Woody," Kat murmured.

"Each letter grew more personal until finally one came in which he asked me to marry him."

"He proposed in a letter?"

"And I accepted in kind," Agnes fired back. "I knew it was a long shot, at best, that anything would really come of the proposal, but I cared about him so much and, well, he was at war asking me to give him something to come home for."

"Wow!" Patsy put her hand to her temple. "What a complex position to be in."

"Complex? That was nothing. Wait until you hear the big finish." Agnes put her hands in her lap and raised her chin, looking as regal as a queen holding court. "When the war ended I got the letter of a lifetime. Woodrow Pennington was coming home."

"Hurray!" Maggie cheered.

Mac nudged her. "You knew he came home."

"I don't care, it's still exciting."

"It was exciting for me too, and overwhelming. You see, he asked me in that letter to meet him when his ship came in and to bring my parents and a bridal bouquet."

"He wanted to m-marry you on the spot?" Even Henry had been ensnared by the drama.

"No, he wanted me to carry the bouquet so he could pick me out of the crowd. As for my parents coming along, he didn't think his future wife should be meeting a battleship unescorted." She laughed. "And he wanted to ask them for my hand in marriage . . . if, after meeting in person, we still wanted to get married. If not . . ."

"What?" Maggie sat up. "If not, then what?"

"If, after we met and spent the day together, if we *both* didn't feel the way we did in our letters, we would part as friends and never contact each other again."

"Oh dear. It must have been so difficult to decide that." Patsy wrung her hands.

"Well, let me put your mind at ease, dear. Love made it easy. I knew that man. I knew his heart. I knew him from a distance and in a crowd of thousands."

"You *knew* him." Kat looked at Eggy.

"And I knew I wanted to take a lifetime getting to know more about him. He got off that ship that morning and I was his wife by nightfall."

"Good thing you brought that bouquet," Patsy spoke up.

Agnes laughed and smiled sweetly. "We had our ups and downs along the way, but those were not because of our unconventional beginnings." Agnes dipped her head slightly toward Eggy and Kat.

They shared a glance, and then smiled at her.

"And mark my words. There was never a stage of our marriage in all of our sixty years that we did not feel the need for love and support of others." The older woman turned her attention then to Henry and Patsy, Mac and Maggie and finally to Louise. "Even when a newlywed came to my home to ask for advice, those glimpses into the larger circle of life, the privilege of watching a new family grow, of seeing love mature, those things helped me as much as my counsel helped you, Louise."

"Sometimes the teacher becomes the student," Louise summed up as she reached out to take Agnes' hand.

"I totally take it back. Every last bit of it." Eggy held up both hands in mock surrender.

"What are you t-talking a-a-about?"

"When I said we wondered if this weekend was all worth it. I take back any doubts I had. This weekend was totally awesome. This night was worth everything."

"You're all right, kid." Mac gave the younger man the thumbs-up sign. "And I'm with you. Only I got a lot more than just this evening to make this weekend worthwhile. I have to admit it, I've learned a lot. A lot of it from you, Eggy."

"Why, Mac, sweetie! You sound suspiciously like a man who might just be open to . . . maybe . . . a little bit . . ." Maggie held her thumb and forefinger apart to illustrate, ". . . of change?"

"Let's start small." He held his thumb and forefinger much closer together than his wife had. "Okay?"

"How?" Maggie expected a verbal commitment.

"How?" Mac stroked his chin. "How about we set up a regular time to get together with our mentorees, no, strike that, with our new *friends*, the Wickhams?"

Maggie looked at the younger couple.

"Cool!" Eggy took Mac's hand and shook it.

"Cool, indeed," Louise murmured, knowing she had just seen the Lord at work.

Louise played "As Time Goes By" again and then another song and then another as the couples gathered around the piano and sang with enthusiasm. In fact, so pleased were they that they hardly even noticed when the lights came back on.

Finally, Henry declared that he had to get some rest to be ready for church the following day. Louise insisted that he and Patsy use a guest bedroom and not brave the walk home. Soon everyone was settled for the night.

In her bedroom, Louise took a moment before doing her nightly Bible reading to gaze at a photo of her dear Eliot and whisper, "I bet there's some boogie-woogie, piano-pounding rejoicing in heaven tonight."

Then she turned her attention to her prayers, remembering Alice and Jane and hoping they would all be ready for whatever the next day would bring.

Chapter Twenty-One

J ane sat at the kitchen table early Sunday morning sipping coffee, refreshed and ready for anything . . . that was, until *anything* came her way.

"Jane? This is Clark. Sorry to call so early on a Sunday morning but I wanted to try to catch you before you started off for church." The clipped harried tone of the usually unflappable contractor was an alarm bell.

"That's all right, Clark. It's not *that* early. Aunt Ethel and I got caught in the storm and had to stay at Sylvia Songer's house last night. But we got up early this morning, saw that the roads were clear and drove back to the inn. Aunt Ethel is already calling people, organizing a phone tree to make sure everyone knows we're holding our service later than usual today because of the road conditions."

Shortly after they had arrived home, Rev. Thompson had called to let them know about the service and to ask Ethel to start the phone tree. While ice on the roads had begun to melt as soon as the sun warmed it, fallen trees and tree limbs had to be attended to before people would be able to move about the town again.

"The idea is to have a shortened service and then to use the church as a base from which to organize people to go out and help their neighbors."

"I hope you count me as your neighbor then, because I sure do need your help."

"That doesn't sound good. What can I do? Was your house damaged in the storm?"

"No, my house is fine. It's my business and reputation that are on the line here."

"Your business? Your reputation? What do you mean, Clark?"

"Lyndon Sturgis is causing trouble."

"What's he doing?"

"Apparently he stormed into the hardware store yesterday afternoon and announced to everyone in earshot that I had acted in a negligent and cavalier way by not finishing in a timely manner the job he had hired me to do."

"No!"

"I'm afraid so. Fred called me and filled me in. And, with many folks in town fearing the worst about the weather, you can just imagine how many people were there to hear all about it."

The day went downhill from there.

"I don't think it's a good idea for us to take a trip across roads that might still have patches of ice and through places that might have ice damage," Louise concluded not long after Jane's conversation with Clark.

Louise had found her sister in the kitchen putting away the clean dishes from the dishwasher while the inn's guests got ready for church upstairs.

"We didn't plan on leaving until after two, so shouldn't everything be clear by then?"

Louise reached over and turned on the small television on the counter.

"We have our eye on a new front moving across the upper northwest of our state with high winds, record cold and the possibility of significant snow accumulations." The weatherman stood in front of a map of a region hundreds of miles away while animated blobs of white and pink moved over the outlines of the states.

"See?" Louise said.

"If we don't go, how will Alice get home?"

"We'll have to go later in the week, weather permitting," Louise decreed. "In fact, we should get this all sorted out before we leave for church."

Jane did not mind making the drive. In truth, she had been looking forward to the time on the return trip with her sisters. She also had been glad for the chance, after she had spoken to Clark, to get away from the Lyndon Sturgis fiasco. She needed some distance both literally and figuratively and longed for whatever perspective Louise and Alice might give her on dealing with Lyndon.

In the past, Jane had felt herself to be independent of her sisters, a person who was not defined solely by her small-town upbringing. She had spent time making a wonderful life for herself in San Francisco. Now, however, with the experience of running the inn and the satisfaction of reconnecting with her roots, Jane had to admit that she did not simply love her sisters, she admired them and she relied on them.

She, who liked to tackle new things, understood as she faced this new wrinkle in her latest undertaking that even those who step up to take charge of helping others sometimes need help themselves.

She leaned one hip against the counter. "I don't have a problem doing the driving, Louise. Maybe if we—"

Louise turned so that Jane could see that she had the phone receiver to her ear and held a finger raised to her lips to show she needed quiet to hear. "Hello? Alice? Yes. We're fine here. We have a broken window but Mac says he can board it up properly this afternoon and that should do until we get an insurance adjuster to come out."

"A window?" Jane didn't know about that.

"In the sunroom," Louise answered Jane and Alice at the same time.

Jane left the kitchen to check out the damage in the sunroom. By the time she returned, Louise had hung up the phone. Louise excused herself to finish getting ready for church and headed out the door.

"So, we're definitely not going to meet Alice and Virginia today?" Jane called after her sister.

"Not today," Louise confirmed. "If you have something else you want to get done, go ahead and plan on it."

"I thought I would find you here, Clark." Jane had driven carefully to Lyndon's lot after church. "I hoped I also might find Lyndon and we could get this all sorted out."

"He left a message on my answering machine, while I was at church. He stayed in Merriville last night but plans to be out here around three."

"Is that all he had to say?"

"He kept it brief, of course. No explanation, no tirades, just the demand that I meet him here then."

Jane nodded. "I was supposed to be out of town most of this afternoon, but since that's been canceled, I can come by then too."

"Thanks, but we don't need a referee, if that's what you're thinking."

"I'm thinking I owe it to both of you to see if I can help smooth things over."

"It may be too late for that, Jane. I had a few other messages on my answering machine from people who'd been at the hardware store telling me that they had heard his outburst." Clark shifted his big work boots over the cold, hard ground and hunched his shoulders in his heavy corduroy coat. "They all were sure to add that they did not believe a word of it."

"Do you know what he said, exactly?"

"That I was negligent for having accepted a job I obviously had not intended to give my full attention, for starters."

"But you had told him you were working him in as you could. He knew that and had several other contractors' names to choose from if he didn't find your terms reasonable." Jane shook her head, amazed that Lyndon could have come to such a flawed conclusion. "What else did he say?"

"That my delays meant they could not get the foundation poured before this bad weather. He said that he had hired the crew that brought in the dirt and gravel and got the ground ready. He claims I balked at pouring the foundation, and now when his kit arrives, he will have to pay an extra day's wages because the crew is scheduled to come out but will only be able to do some preliminary work."

"You told him you weren't happy with the way the ground was prepped, didn't you?"

"He says that was done according to my instructions, so I should take responsibility for that."

"You have, by *not* going ahead with laying the foundation. It seems to me, if nothing else, the storm that blew through here last night should be evidence that you made a sound decision." It all seemed so straightforward to Jane.

"Yes, and our friends and neighbors here in Acorn Hill understand that, but I have a bad feeling that Lyndon may not be just venting his unhappiness locally. He has been staying in Merriville, after all."

"Oh dear. You are probably right, Clark."

"That he is saying these things in Merriville?"

"No, that Lyndon is spreading his unhappiness. I know it's not fair to you, but I can't help thinking that this has more to do with his grief over the loss of his wife than his steadfast belief that you have actually done him any disservice."

"You're probably right, but it certainly doesn't help my reputation."

Jane unfastened her coat. The temperatures had not risen drastically, but the sun had come out, making it feel warmer and causing the ice to melt rapidly.

All around them the steady *plop plop plop* of water dripping off branches and hitting the slower-to-thaw ground sounded like a ticking clock. That image only served to remind her of what a hurry Lyndon was always in and Ethel's warning about how haste ended up costing people time and money in the long run.

"But he has all the paperwork, step by step, where I told him what to do and says he did as I instructed." Clark shook his head. "In the end, I am the contractor. The customer feels I didn't do my job. I feel I have to accept some responsibility for that."

"You are an honorable man, Clark. That's the way everyone in town who knows you or has done business with you feels about you." She had to look up to speak to him. The brilliant sun shone in her eyes and she shaded them as she said, "No one in Acorn Hill would believe for a minute that you would ever be careless or negligent on any of your jobs."

"Thank you, Jane. I came out here today to see what I could figure out, to see if there is something I can do to get this place ready for when Lyndon's A-frame kit arrives."

"If it warms up today, could you pour the foundation soon?"

He looked up at the sky, frowned and sighed. "I suppose maybe I could, but, well, I just don't see how it would help things. I would rather take my lumps and make it right than rush and risk making things worse."

"What are you going to do now?"

"I've gone over all my orders and double-checked with

the crew Lyndon hired. At this point I want to do a visual on the place as best I can under these conditions. I know the footer wall—the foundation's foundation, as it were—was solid. The gravel was—"

"The gravel!" Jane reached into her coat pocket and produced the pink piece of paper she had found. "Look here, it seems that there was something up with the gravel."

He took the page from her. "It's from the crew who hauled the fill dirt and gravel to the site."

"Yes, and it's got Lyndon's name on the top as the buyer, but he didn't sign it."

"I appreciate your thinking here, but this looks like it was just a mistake." He handed the invoice back to her. "You can see the ink marks where it's been altered, crossed through and then ultimately had the word 'void' at the top."

Jane squinted at the pale blue letters and sighed. "When I first saw all the marks on the receipt, I thought: That's business with Lyndon, he'd try to make you renegotiate your own name if he thought the way you spelled it wasted too much of his time writing it out."

Clark chuckled. Then he rubbed his forehead and mused, "Believe me. I've thought this through from every angle."

"But when it thaws a little, maybe you can tell better what the problem is."

"I suspect when I finally see Lyndon, he'll be telling me I'm off the job. I won't have another chance to see what's gone on. That's why I'm out here now." He gazed at the site and shook his head. "In all my years, I've never been fired from a job, Jane. I wish I knew how to reason with Lyndon so we could come to an agreement to make this right."

"Well, then we'll have to dig around a little."

"Dig? The ground is still frozen."

"I mean to do the kind of digging around that doesn't require a shovel." Jane studied the scene, and then put her hand in her pocket, touching the paper she had tucked away. "I got you into this. I should make an effort to help you out of it."

"I don't see how you can."

"For openers, with your permission, I can talk to Lyndon."

"Fine. As I said, he should be out here later today. I have to leave to make the rounds seeing how I can help people with storm damage until then."

"I'll come by around three then."

"You think you can talk sense into him?"

"Ah, *sense* might be a little overambitious."

"You'd have better luck talking dollars and cents," Clark muttered.

The truth of his words resonated with Jane. Whatever was at the bottom of it, though, Jane had some time to try to unearth it.

Chapter Twenty-Two

"I can't believe how quickly things can turn around!" Patsy Ley met Jane coming in the door to the inn as Patsy was heading out, carrying a box of scrapbooking materials.

"I, um . . ." Jane did not get a chance to respond to her statement as Patsy hurried off. Jane looked at Louise, who stood in the foyer having accompanied the associate pastor's wife to the door. "What did she mean by that? That things turn around so quickly? Was she talking about something that happened during your weekend event?"

Louise shut the door and shrugged. "I suppose she could have been. Or about the weather. Or about Alice's news."

"Whoa! Wait!" Jane threw up her hand. "Alice has news? What news?"

"About that little baby born on New Year's Day. She got word from the hospital that he's going home."

"That's wonderful."

"Yes, and what's more, his parents have relented and contacted their families for help. With them for emotional support and the money the hospital has raised, thanks in no small part to Alice's efforts, they should be fine."

"Terrific. I needed to hear some good news this afternoon."

"Well, there you have it. Of course, she could have meant Alice's other good news."

"Louise!"

Louise laughed. "It's nothing huge. It's just that Mark checked with the highway department and they gave the all clear for the drive."

"We're going?" She started to put her coat back on.

"Not us." Louise held up her hand to stop Jane. "Mark has kindly offered to drive Alice here today and then he and Mrs. Pennington will head back to Philadelphia tomorrow, weather permitting."

"Oh. That's nice. It will be good to see Mark. And I have plenty to keep me occupied here."

"Yes, Lyndon's project." Louise headed off toward the kitchen.

"You know about that?" Jane knew Louise had been all but sequestered in the house the day before. And she hadn't heard anyone mention the scene in the hardware store at church. Not that she expected people to talk about it. The storm was the major topic of conversation, and it was not in the nature of her neighbors to gossip about something they knew to be unfounded. "What have you heard?" she asked as she followed Louise into the kitchen.

"Heard?" Louise looked puzzled. "Jane, I've known you were helping the man since he called and asked you to do it." Louise went to the pantry, took out a box of cat food and shook it as a sort of dinner bell for Wendell, their tabby cat. "The house plans have been in Father's study since before they began to clear and level the land."

"Oh, right. Sorry about that."

"Oh, that was no problem. I know you had to have a firm, flat spot to lay them out."

"Well, true as that is, I'm sorry that I didn't put them away for the weekend. I'll go get them in a minute and put them where they won't be in the way any longer. I'm not sure if I'll need to look at them anymore. I suspect that Lyndon and I may have a parting of the ways soon."

"Really?"

"Well, if you don't mind, I'll not talk about that right now. Things are still up in the air."

"Certainly, dear. No need to borrow trouble."

Jane bent down to pick up Wendell's dish from the floor. She handed it to Louise and then hung her coat on a hook by the door. Louise poured the dry food into the bowl and then gave the box another shake.

"Where *is* Wendell?" Jane asked.

"As far as I can tell, he went into hiding at the height of the storm, probably when the tree branch went through the window."

"That sounds like him."

"I wanted to make sure he's all right. I went looking for him after church. Called him. Checked to make sure none of our guests shut him up in a closet or room. Agnes keeps telling me he'll show himself when he gets hungry enough."

"So you thought you'd help that hunger along with an uncustomary afternoon snack?"

"One thing I learned this weekend, Jane, was that creatures of habit sometimes need to be coaxed into doing what's best for them."

As if out of thin air, the cat appeared, purring and winding his way around the women's ankles.

Louise bent and set down the grateful cat's bowl. "What's this?"

She straightened again with the pink receipt from Lyndon's lot in her hand.

"That must have fallen out of my pocket." Jane whisked it away but then at the sight of her own handwriting remembered the notation she had promised to ask Louise about. "I made some notes on it, and one of them was to ask you about a quote that I think is from C. S. Lewis."

"Excellent." Louise took a seat and folded her hands

looking like a contestant on a quiz show ready to face her challenge.

Jane unfolded the paper, glancing first at the side with the information from the dirt and gravel company and then at her handwriting on the other side. "I don't know it exactly but it's something like—'Prayer does not change things, it changes us.'"

"*Hmm.* It is the kind of topic Lewis liked to take on, but I think the quote you are thinking of is from Søren Kierkegaard. 'Prayer does not change God but changes him who prays.'"

"That could be it but said that way it doesn't quite seem to fit what I was thinking of." Jane sat down at the table.

"I've also heard it said, though I have never found a source for it, that prayer doesn't change things, it changes people and people then take actions that change things."

"That's more what I had in mind." Jane flattened out the paper. "I feel that's what happened when we decided to heed the sermon on service and volunteered in prayer to report to duty."

"Yes, exactly."

"Then I think about Lyndon and how I've prayed for him, that he would find contentment here and that the job would go well, and, well, I don't see any change in him at all." Jane thought of how he had dwelt on the matter of time and money from the very first day she'd spoken to him on the phone. That certainly hadn't changed.

For a few moments she thought back over her interaction with the man. She pictured the tall Texan showing off his many technological gadgets and shook her head at his penchant for not listening when he was in a hurry to get things done. She mused about how that drive to get things done often meant he would charge ahead and do the work he had asked her to do and how Aunt Ethel had warned that would cost him time in the long run. She thought of how sweetly he spoke of his wife and daughter and how he had said that he would not expect any man to do work that he would not do . . . "Himself," she whispered.

"What?"

"This receipt." Jane flipped over the paper in her hand, and then flipped it again to show it to Louise. "It's not about changing the dirt or gravel order. It's about Lyndon costing himself in the long run because he didn't want to pay for overtime."

"Jane, you are not making any sense."

"I'm sorry. I can't tell you the details just now." She went to the coat hook, grabbed her coat and hurried off, calling good-bye to her sister before she hurried out the door.

"Have you ever heard the adage 'penny-wise and pound-foolish'?" Jane called out to the men standing toe to toe between their vehicles, which sat parked bumper to bumper.

Both Clark and Lyndon turned their heads to look at her as she got out of her car.

The wind whipped at her ponytail. She shut her car door and it echoed against the pine trees at the back of the cleared lot a hundred feet away.

"Well, it seems to me that your foolishness can be measured in tons instead of pounds, Lyndon."

"Doesn't that saying refer to English pounds? Money?" Lyndon asked, tipping his hat to her as she reached his side. "Though it is good to see you, ma'am, I don't see how this is your fight."

Jane let the polite-but-grating *ma'am* slide. He hadn't meant to needle her, and she would not let his words do so. "No, of course not. It is not my fight. I hope it's no one's fight. This is the kind of situation you deal with by talking, reasoning, apologizing, but not fighting."

"Oh, I've accepted Mr. Barrett's apology, all right. Now we just have to decide what it is he is going to do to compensate me for my loss of time and money."

Coaxing. Creatures of habit need coaxing, she reminded herself of Louise's observation.

"I think you are getting a little ahead of yourself, Lyndon." Jane offered both men a pleasant smile and then pulled the pink receipt from her pocket. "I believe this is yours."

Lyndon glanced down and then waved his hand to dismiss it. "That was voided. It's trash."

"That's probably why I found it in with the rest of the rubble you used instead of fill dirt." Jane looked at Clark.

"What?" the contractor asked.

"How much time do you suppose it would save if, instead of hauling away brush, you dug a hole, buried it and then packed down the displaced dirt from the hole on top of it?" Jane slid the paper from Lyndon's fingers and presented it to Clark. "This isn't voided because of an issue with gravel. This was voided because Lyndon cut the amount of fill dirt he ordered."

Clark looked at her and then at Lyndon. "How did you talk one of my crews into doing something like that?"

"I didn't. When they went home at quitting time, I was out here by myself. The clock was ticking. Time is—"

"Oh, Lyndon." Jane cut him off with a shake of her head. "You have just cost yourself so much of both time *and* money."

"Nobody ever told me *not* to do it," he blustered. "I let the crew do the work on the important part of the land, I just thought, over here, where it would just be grass and side yard, it wouldn't matter. I think you're just grasping at straws to cover up Barrett's mistakes."

"Lyndon!" Jane was shocked at the remark.

"I wish there were a way to make you see this," Clark

said. "I reminded you about the lay of the land when we first came out to the lot and I pointed out to you the possibility of what's happening now, but I can't really show you what will happen over time and if you won't believe me—"

"Wait." Jane had an idea about how Clark might illustrate his point. "Lyndon, you've taken pictures every step of the way to send to your daughter, haven't you?"

"You know I have."

Jane looked at Clark.

"That would be most helpful," he told her.

"Would you mind giving us a little slide show, Lyndon?" Jane knew she wouldn't have to ask twice. The man loved showing off his gadgets almost as much as he loved saving money.

He set his laptop on the hood of his SUV and after a few clicks, they were looking at a photo of the lot on the very first day the two of them had come out to see it.

"There!" Clark used his finger to circle a spot where some bushes grew at odd angles from the side of a very small hill. "That's the way the land was before we did anything to it. See how it has a natural slope to it?"

"Yeah, and we compensated for that by building up the area the house sits on," Lyndon said in a stubborn tone as he made another click and showed a picture further in the process.

"Now, look at the lay of your foundation." Clark pointed to the back corner of the frame his crew had put in place on Friday. Look at the slope starting a few feet out from it."

"So?" Lyndon looked from the photo on his laptop to the side of his plot of land.

"Now go back to the first shot." Clark gestured to the screen and when Lyndon obeyed, he pointed to the photo. "You have built up that area but not enough to compensate for the amount I had them build up the area for the foundation. You still have a very similar degree of slope."

Lyndon peered first at one photo and then the next. "I don't see it that way."

"Then look at what's happening right in front of you. As the snow and ice melt, they run from the high spot that was correctly built up for your A-frame toward the places where you used the brush and debris as filler."

Jane and Lyndon followed the line of Clark's hand as Clark spelled out the situation.

"Now consider years of the run-off of rain and snow flowing that way, eroding the top soil and there being nothing underneath. What do you imagine will happen?"

Lyndon narrowed his eyes. "So I have a few sinkholes in my side yard. I don't see how that matters."

"Not even if your new grandchild was playing in that side yard?" Jane asked.

Even in the shade of his cowboy hat, Lyndon's face went visibly paler.

"And nothing happens in and of itself, Lyndon. Those sinkholes and irregularities wouldn't be limited to just a few spots, they would have an effect on the whole lot, causing your foundation to settle, perhaps even crack. That could cause cracks in the walls, mold growth. In time your sleeping loft might not even be safe and would have to be redone entirely." Clark put his hands on his hips. He did not seem forbidding or angry, but anxious to make sure Lyndon understood the situation. "You may have saved yourself a few hours of overtime and a ton of dirt, but in the long run you could have cost yourself ten times as much."

"That's not even the real cost here, Lyndon." Jane stepped up. "Because of your blind spot about time and money, you were willing to tarnish the reputation of a good contractor, a good man. That's not the kind of thing you can put a price on."

Lyndon pushed his cowboy hat to the back of his head. Red-cheeked and stunned, he blew out air from his rounded lips. "I have to think about this. Mind if I take a walk around for a minute or two?"

"You take as long as you need, Lyndon. There's nothing more for me to do here today. But if you still want me in charge of your build, call me. I would like to see this through if at all possible." Clark held his hand out to Lyndon.

"I have to say one thing. If I could do it over, I'd have never spoken out against you in public like that." Lyndon took the man's hand. It was not an apology but it was a step toward a peace offering. "That was unkind and uncalled for." Another step.

"Thank you for that much." Clark gave Jane a nod to say good-bye and then turned, got in his truck and drove off.

"You probably think that wasn't nearly good enough." Lyndon looked at her, sheepishly. "But I meant it, every word."

"I think if you really mean it, you'll say it in the same place you chose to impugn Clark's integrity and work ethic."

"I suppose you're right. I'll rectify that first thing in the morning." Lyndon looked at the frame for the foundation. "But that doesn't mean I believe I am wrong about this. It's going to take a lot longer to get this project finished now, and that's not up for debate by anyone."

"Yes, it will take time, but most things that are worthwhile do take time, Lyndon. Why wouldn't you want to take as long as you need to get this project done right? After all, it *is* your home."

"No, it's a house, Jane. Just a house," he corrected gently even as he turned his gaze on her. "Without Barbie, it will never be a home. No matter what I do, no matter how much I try to make things new and different, it will always just be the house that I built without her by my side."

Jane hated to see the heavy burden of sadness that settled over him as he spoke. She tipped her head to one side, enabling her better to see into his downcast eyes as she suggested, "Have you ever thought that, in time, it will become the house that your grandchild—or even grandchildren—think of as Grandpa's home?"

He lifted his head and a twinkle of light returned to his eyes. "I hadn't thought of that." He inhaled a deep breath and then took a few steps. He scanned the area, squinted, then turned and said to her over his shoulder, "You know, I really do owe it to that next generation to make sure Grandpa's home doesn't fall apart just because he was too eager to get it put up, too cheap to pay for the proper workmanship and too stubborn to admit when he was wrong."

Jane smiled. "Does that mean you're going to apologize to Clark and follow his advice from here on out?"

"I will apologize and in public." Lyndon gave her a nod. "I can take my medicine. I just hope that after the way I acted, y'all still want me as your neighbor."

"I guess I can speak for most of 'us-all' and say that the people of Acorn Hill would love having you for our neighbor, Lyndon."

"I am awfully sorry over this mess and the way I acted to Clark and to you too, Jane. Do you really think folks around here could learn to put up with a, uh, cost-conscious Texan a few months out of the year?"

"Yes. As long as that Texan remembers that time is not money. Time is the stuff of life, and life, at least here in Acorn Hill, is worth spending with one another." Jane extended her hand. "Welcome, neighbor."

Chapter Twenty-Three

"Now, let me get this straight—we are not allowed to sing 'Auld Lang Syne' anytime but at midnight on New Year's Eve." Ethel sat in the parlor with her hands folded on top of a throw pillow so that everyone could see the beautiful manicure Sylvia and Jane had given her during their do-it-yourself spa day.

"There is no prohibition about when you sing the song, Aunt Ethel." Louise rose from the piano bench in order to shuffle through a collection of music she had gathered up.

"I think people should sing whatever they want, *when*ever they want. Music keeps your heart young," Agnes observed. "People should do more singing."

"I agree, though I thought you were more in favor of people trying new things, like surfing the Web," Ethel said.

"Who says you can't do both?" Agnes grinned. "Some people whistle while they work, I sing while I surf."

When Louise and Agnes had told Ethel and Jane about their sing-along during the power outage, both of them thought it was such a fun idea that they suggested they have one too. So Louise had collected some songs she felt they would all know.

Jane had started homemade soups, potato and tomato,

simmering in the kitchen. The aroma filled the inn. She planned on making grilled cheese sandwiches with thick-cut bread and Gruyère from Switzerland to serve with the soups as soon as Alice and Mark arrived from Philadelphia.

The weather had grown progressively colder through the day until even the sunshine could not take off the chill. Still, the closeness of friends and family warmed her quite nicely, Louise decided. She searched through the stack of music and tugged free the old book of Christmas carols that had once belonged to her dear Eliot.

"'Auld Lang Syne' it is," she announced as she settled back down and flipped to the proper page.

Louise had barely struck the first chord when the front door opened.

"*Brrrr.*" Ethel feigned a shiver even though they could only hear the winter wind, not feel it.

And with that wind came Alice's cheery, "Hello! We're here!"

"I have come to return the world-renowned public speaker to her loving family," Mark called out.

"We're in the parlor." Jane went to the doorway. "Come in and warm yourselves by the fire. We're singing a few songs before we eat."

Mark waved to the gathering in the parlor, his kindly face bright from the cold.

Louise did the honors of introducing Agnes to Mark as the newly arrived pair slipped out of their winter gear.

"Sorry we weren't here sooner." Alice took her guest's coat and her own. "We made a detour to Potterston to see Baby New Year just in case he goes home before I work my next shift, and guess what?"

"You gave them your check and they named the baby after you?" Ethel clapped her hands in delight at her own inspired conclusion.

"You're right about the checks. I had one from Rachel Grissom and her company to donate as well as my own and I did drop them off."

"Aunt Ethel, it's a boy baby," Jane reminded her aunt. "They wouldn't name a boy Alice."

"But they *did* name him." Alice set aside the coats so she could use both hands to gesture as she shared the news. "And it's the best thing. Pure coincidence, I know, but still, just perfect."

"What did they name him?" Louise was literally on the edge of her seat.

"They named this wonderful new baby, who has his whole life stretching out before him and the love of his family surrounding him . . . they named him Daniel."

"Daniel," Ethel looked as if she might dissolve into tears. "Your father's name."

Alice walked over and gave their aunt a hug. Then she motioned for Mark to take a seat. "I believe you said you were having a sing-along?"

Louise turned back to the keyboard, but couldn't quite make herself play the song before her.

Ethel sniffled. "All of a sudden I understand completely what you mean about 'Auld Lang Syne,' Louise. It is awfully sentimental. I don't think I could take singing it now."

"I agree," Jane echoed the feeling. "We need something that speaks to the kind of month we've just had—all of us busy with new things, following through on new commitments."

"Learning to cherish our foundations because they give us our futures," Alice said.

"Remembering that love is the greatest constant of all," Agnes said quietly.

"Then I know just what we should sing." With those words Louise launched into the song that Woodrow Pennington had sung for his sweetheart. The song Eggy and

Kat had taken on as their own after learning it by the fire in this very room. A song that was to Louise sentimental, but so hopeful that one couldn't help but feel uplifted.

When the last strains of the piano faded and the Howard sisters, Ethel and the rest of the group had sung the last words of "As Time Goes By," Agnes Pennington summed up for them the whole width and breadth of all they had learned during the month and all they had just celebrated in song by adding in a firm and exuberant voice, "And that isn't poppycock!"

New Year's Day Hoppin' John

1½ cups dry black-eyed peas
2 small ham hocks or a meaty ham bone
   or 2 cups diced ham
1 medium onion, chopped
1 celery stalk, chopped
1 green pepper, chopped
1 red pepper, chopped
Bay leaf
4 cups chicken broth
2 cloves of garlic, halved
3 dashes liquid smoke or hot sauce or
   cayenne pepper to taste (optional)
1½ cups long-grain white rice
Salt and pepper

Put all of the ingredients, except the rice, in a large pot. Bring to a boil. Cover pot and reduce heat to medium-low and cook for ninety minutes.

Remove the ham hock or bone, dice the meat and return the meat to the pot. Stir in the rice, cover and cook on low heat until rice is tender, about twenty to twenty-five minutes. Season to taste with salt and pepper.

Serve with corn bread.

About the Author

Annie Jones has been creating stories since she can remember and was first published a decade ago. Her books have won awards for Southern fiction and have been Alternate Selections for Literary Guild, Doubleday and Crossings book clubs. She lives with her husband and two children in rural Kentucky, where she is learning the ins and outs of country life.

A Note from the Editors

This original book was created by the Books and Inspirational Media Division of Guideposts, the world's leading inspirational publisher. Founded in 1945 by Dr. Norman Vincent Peale and Ruth Stafford Peale, Guideposts helps people from all walks of life achieve their maximum personal and spiritual potential. Guideposts is committed to communicating positive, faith-filled principles for people everywhere to use in successful daily living.

Our publications include award-winning magazines such as *Guideposts* and *Angels on Earth*, best-selling books, and outreach services that demonstrate what can happen when faith and positive thinking are applied in day-to-day life.

For more information, visit us at www.guideposts.com, call (800) 431-2344 or write Guideposts, PO Box 5815, Harlan, Iowa 51593.